Loving Ilsa

Alicia Wiggins

Marvelous Words Publishing PO Box 28928

Columbus, OH 43228

CHAPTER ONE

"You did it, girl!"

"I don't know if I can take all the credit. Besides, is *it* ever really over? Doesn't feel that way."

"Honey, as of this past Saturday your last child is officially a married man and out of your house. He is no longer your responsibility. The nest is empty. The apron strings have been cut. So yes, it is over."

Ilsa thought about her best friend Denita's declaration. She was right. Her youngest son was now married and would be living a life in which he no longer needed the care, protection, and attention of his mother. Truth be told, he hadn't needed those things from her in quite a while.

"You know what this means, don't you?"

Ilsa shook her head and patiently waited for a dose of Denita's sage advice.

"Not only is it appropriate to celebrate, but it's also time for you to start living again as a carefree woman with no dependents at home. You're free! You need to go out, throw caution to the wind, have fun, get a man."

Stalling as she tried to come up with a snappy comeback, Ilsa glanced around the crowded restaurant and then back at her well-meaning friend. If she had a dollar for every time Denita gave her that piece of advice, she'd have a whole lot of dollars. Even when her boys were at home, Denita constantly urged Ilsa to go out and have some adult fun. Over the past few years, she had added the "get a man" part to her perceived formula for Ilsa's happiness.

"Dee, you know I love you. Over the years I have leaned on you, vented to and with you, and laughed and cried with you. There have been countless bottles of wine, greasy pizzas, and cartons of ice cream shared between us—more than I care to admit—but seriously, I don't know why you keep telling me the same thing."

"Because you won't listen and, for some reason, you refuse to take my advice. Instead, you work late every evening, take work home with you on the weekends, and continuously put your staff's needs ahead of your own. And I can't remember the last time you had a date or even got dressed up and treated yourself to a nice dinner or a concert. You live like an eighty-year-old spinster." Denita ignored the exaggerated frown on her friend's face. "Need I remind you that you're a forty-five-year-old single woman who is extremely brilliant, absolutely beautiful, amazingly funny, remarkably successful, and sexy as hell?"

"I need to hire you as my PR rep. But you do have one thing wrong. I am living, thank you very much."

"No, no." Denita wagged her finger. "Don't mistake what you're doing with living. My cat has more of an active social life than you."

Ilsa finished her glass of wine and poured another. Hesitating before taking a sip, she looked thoughtfully at her friend. After all these years, Denita continued to look out for her best interests. However much she disagreed with her approach, admittedly she might be on to something. The prospect of shaking a few things up in her life might not be so terrible.

"Does that mean you agree?" Denita asked, already anticipating a favorable answer.

"Dee, I know I need to get out of the house and do more than just work. I've been on that track for a long time. Don't get me wrong. I still love my job, with the exception of Grant, but since the kids have grown up, gotten married, and moved away, I guess I should start looking at being more Ilsa and less Mom. I have to admit the concept is a little foreign to me at the moment. I'm going to need some coaching."

Excited that she had finally breached the steel wall of resistance, Denita raised her glass. "Hear, hear! I say let's toast to new and exciting adventures."

Laughing, the two clinked their glasses and finished their wine.

"So, what do you think you'll do first? Sign up on a dating site? Buy a sexy sports car? Oh, I know. You should look into one of those singles-only cruises."

Laughing at the barrage of corny suggestions, Ilsa responded in the most responsible tone she could muster. "I've been on vacation for almost a week getting ready for and then recovering from the wedding. The first order of business is to get back to work so I can continue to have a job to pay for all of the crazy activities you want me to indulge in. By the way, the car thing, that's a big, fat, no. If I can't be sexy and interesting in the car I have, then too bad."

Denita shrugged. "Baby steps."

They finished their dinner and moved on to other topics of conversation.

"Wow, my food was amazing. Yours looked good too. Maybe I'll order that when I come back. Good idea suggesting we come here for dinner."

Denita nodded. "This place has been open for almost three years. I've been meaning to stop in and check it out, but it's always so busy. When you called and said you didn't feel like cooking, this was the first place I thought of. Glad we were able to get in."

Ilsa looked around the busy restaurant. In addition to good food and an inviting atmosphere, the service had been excellent. Featuring Greek and Mediterranean dishes, locally sourced ingredients, and seasonal entrees, all of which had sounded interesting to her, she had readily agreed to Denita's suggestion. Since turning forty she decided to be more open to trying new things. With this choice, she certainly wasn't disappointed.

While they were deciding on whether to indulge in dessert, the waiter appeared at their table. The young man with dark eyes, heavily moussed hair, and deep dimples smiled and placed a small sampling of desserts on their table.

"Oh, we didn't order—" Denita began.

"It's on the house," he replied and left as quickly as he had appeared.

Denita and Ilsa looked at each other and smiled.

"I *really* like this restaurant," Denita remarked.

As they sampled the baklava, cake, and little pastries that neither of them could name but loved just the same, they momentarily forgot about calories and sensible eating.

"Are you enjoying the desserts?"

Expecting to see their waiter, they were surprised to see someone else. A very handsome someone else. Always quick on her feet, Denita responded first.

"Yes, everything was delicious."

Ilsa wasn't sure if her friend was talking about the dessert or the handsome man who had just appeared at their table. Well-built with thick dark hair that was slightly more salt than pepper at the temples, he wore a pale yellow dress shirt paired with dark-washed jeans, unlike the wait staff who wore white shirts and black pants. Although casually dressed he was still quite put together. Olive-skinned with just the hint of a five o'clock shadow, his dark eyes were hidden under thick but not unruly brows. Ilsa noticed a slight smile curling his lips. She found herself staring, something that was completely out character for her.

"And you?" he asked, looking directly at Ilsa. "Did you enjoy the desserts?"

"Uh, yes, I...I did," she said, a little surprised he had addressed her directly. Had he caught her staring?

"I'm glad. We love satisfied customers," he replied with a smile meant just for her. "I'm Dominic Markos."

"The owner," Denita chimed in when she recognized the name, knowing her friend had no idea who this handsome man was.

Dominic nodded and smiled self-consciously. "Yes, the owner."

Denita glanced at Ilsa, who clearly was about to let a prime flirting opportunity pass her by. "I'm Denita Harper, and this is my friend Ilsa Tanner."

"It's a pleasure to meet you, ladies," Dominic replied to both women but never took his eyes off Ilsa.

Just then a waitress came over to the table and said something to Dominic about him being needed in the kitchen. He looked slightly annoyed by the interruption, but duty called. Reluctantly, he excused himself.

The moment his back was turned, Denita faced Ilsa with a broad smile.

"What?" Ilsa asked.

"Are you serious? That man was flirting with you big time."

"So?"

"So you could have flirted back."

"Dee, you know I'm not good at flirting. Besides, he's probably married with a house full of kids."

"What makes you say that? I didn't see a ring on his finger."

"That doesn't mean a thing."

Denita leaned back in her seat and frowned. "There's no harm in flirting, Ilsa. You didn't even try."

"Oh, come on. He probably flirts with all of his female customers. With that sexy smile and his good looks, he's trying to guarantee that there's always a full house and plenty of repeat customers."

"Something tells me you might be wrong about that."

Checking her watch, Ilsa noted the time. It was getting late, and she needed to get home.

"Right or wrong, let's get the waiter's attention and get our check. Remember, my first day back to work is tomorrow, and I need to be up early to face whatever impossible demands Grant has in store for me."

"Seriously, Ilsa, I don't know why you don't put your foot down about the way he treats you and the staff."

"Because I'd like to keep my job and not get fired."

Denita spotted their waiter a few tables over, waved to him, and mouthed "check please." He nodded in acknowledgment and walked to the back of the restaurant.

As they waited for the waiter to bring their check, Ilsa and Denita went back and forth about who would be picking up the tab.

"Ilsa, I'm not hearing it. You just helped pay for Byron and Patrice's wedding. Let me take care of the bill tonight. You can treat next time."

When the waiter returned to the table, he placed the bill between the two women, smiled, and walked away before Denita had a chance to give him her credit card.

"What the heck?" she asked. However, when she opened the folder to view the bill she smiled with understanding at his odd behavior.

"What?"

"It's free."

"What's free?"

"Our meal. The whole thing, including the bottle of wine. Look."

Ilsa took the bill and scanned down to the bottom of the page. Sure enough, the total read $0.00. But there was something else. Included with the bill was a business card. The front of the card featured the name of the restaurant, YiaYia's Table, the owner's name, the restaurant's address, and phone number.

"Turn it over," Denita instructed.

On the back was a note:

Ilsa Tanner, please don't let this be the last time I'm allowed to treat you to dinner.

CHAPTER TWO

Ilsa's return to work was more welcomed than she had anticipated, both by herself and her staff. Although she had been busy with her son's wedding, she still missed being at work. Her job at New Hope Family Center, a not-for-profit agency that worked to secure employment, housing, mental health counseling, and other needed services for women who were previously homeless or were facing homelessness, was as fulfilling as it was demanding. Unfortunately, the agency's executive director, Grant Towson, who had been there a little less than a year, routinely made their jobs much harder than was necessary. Rude, demeaning, and completely lacking in empathy, Grant had managed to alienate almost everyone during his short tenure. To counter his toxic behavior and in an effort to help maintain everyone's sanity, Ilsa did her best to act as a buffer between him and the staff whenever possible, often taking the brunt of his ill behavior upon herself.

Grant had been hired by New Hope's board of directors to bring a fresh perspective and new direction to the center. As the associate director, Ilsa had been disappointed when she wasn't promoted to the position when the previous executive director retired. She went along with the board's decision without too much outward objection, although she secretly questioned Grant's appointment once she learned he had previously worked in education as the superintendent of a small school district. In addition to his poor behavior, he had never even worked for a non-profit. To make things more complicated, Grant refused to listen to new ideas, wasn't the least bit interested in staff development, and was frequently in a bad mood.

As the center's associate director, Ilsa's responsibilities included managing the day-to-day activities of the staff, developing the center's programs, and forging community relationships. In reality, she did much more, from grant writing to staff counseling and mentoring to event planning and everything in between. Blessed with an amazing staff who worked as hard as she did to make a difference in the lives of the women they served, she enjoyed what she did and, quite frankly, couldn't see herself doing anything else. Aside from dealing with Grant and his incessant micromanaging, meddling, and bad attitude, her job was almost perfect.

Settling back into a routine after being off work wasn't as difficult as she had anticipated, except for the volume of emails. As she waded through screen after screen of emails that had piled up during her absence, she came across one announcing restaurant week. The event had passed, but she scrolled through the list of restaurants that had offered special menus and extended hours to see if anything was interesting. Then she saw it. YiaYia's Table.

Shifting her attention from the tedious chore of clearing out her inbox to the handsome and slightly more interesting restaurant owner she'd met the night before was an easy transition. She had yet to call to take him up on his offer. She also hadn't made up her mind if she even would or not. Of course, Denita wanted her to jump on his offer immediately. That wasn't quite her style—not that she had any real style to speak of. Sadly, she would never be accused of being overly spontaneous, something she had been meaning to improve. Though, in her defense, until now she hadn't had much room in her life or a lot of extra personal time for dating or spontaneity.

Ilsa's husband, Quinn, had been the love of her life. They had made many plans for the future and their two sons. Sadly, all of that changed when Quinn suffered a heart attack at the age of thirty-nine, leaving Ilsa alone to finish raising their sons and forced to make sense of being a widow at thirty-five.

With two young boys to raise and instantly thrust into the role of a single parent, her personal life had become almost non-existent. When the boys had gotten a little older she tried her hand at dating, but nothing much came of it—neither lasting relationships, interesting friendships, nor passionate affairs.

Ilsa completely gave up on reading emails for a while and took a few minutes to think about how much had changed in her life over the past several years. Her sons were now grown, married, and on their own. The house she had shared with them was no longer cluttered with football gear and teenage boys or filled with the chaotic excitement and brevity of weekends and holidays home from college. Her life had changed, and she needed to change with it.

Denita said it was time for her to reinvent her life. She didn't necessarily agree with her friend, at least not to the extremes she often suggested. She liked who she was. She simply needed to redefine herself, slightly.

Ilsa reached into her purse and retrieved Dominic's business card. She carefully looked it over as if she could tell something about the man or his intentions from the three-by-five-inch piece of cardstock.

Dominic Markos. Hmm...was he Greek? Italian? Something else? His last name was of Greek origin. She only knew that because she looked it up online. His deep olive skin, dark hair, and chiseled features made her wonder what other countries his family tree was rooted in.

Pulled away from her thoughts when her cell phone vibrated, Ilsa saw Denita's name displayed on the screen.

"Hey, Dee. What's up?"

"Did you call him yet?"

"Seriously? That's how you start the conversation?"

"Look, I don't have a lot of time. I'm meeting a client in twenty minutes, and I still have some notes to review. So, back to my question, did you call him yet?"

Denita was about business, matter-of-fact, and the most down-to-earth person she knew. Most of the time Ilsa loved those qualities about her. Today, not so much.

"No, Dee. I haven't called him."

The sound of keys clicking on a computer keyboard let Ilsa know Denita was multitasking, but that didn't mean she didn't have her friend's attention.

"Why not? The man was definitely interested. He's sexy, handsome, gainfully employed, and generous. All good qualities. And my 'this dude might be crazy' sensor didn't trigger any bells or whistles. Trust that we'll dig into that area more thoroughly a little later."

"I don't know, Dee. You of all people know I'm not the kind of woman who chases a man."

Ilsa heard an unmistakable sigh.

"You're aware that it's not 1920, right? It's perfectly acceptable for a woman to pursue a relationship or, at the very least, a date with a man that she finds attractive."

"Did I say I found him attractive?"

"You didn't have to. You practically stared a hole into his soul when he was standing at our table."

Busted!

"Well?"

"I guess you're right," Ilsa reluctantly admitted.

"Of course I am. Now, give him a call, then call me back and let me know what happened."

After she ended the call, Ilsa looked at the phone number again and took a deep breath. *Here's to spontaneity.* Unfortunately, before she could make the call, her admin Priscilla peeked into her office.

"Busy?"

"No," Ilsa replied abruptly, feeling as if she'd been caught doing something wrong.

"Emergency meeting in the conference room. Don't worry. I think we might be getting some good news for a change."

Well, spontaneity would have to wait a little longer.

CHAPTER THREE

"Yes, Mom." Dominic balanced the phone on his shoulder, signed for the produce order, and mouthed "thank you" to the delivery driver.

"Of course, Mom." He nodded to the team chopping vegetables and prepping for the lunch rush as he headed back to his office. Once inside he closed the door, temporarily shutting out the restaurant's sounds and activity that he loved so much.

"Why don't you come out for a while? I don't like you being so far away with no one to look after you."

Dominic and his sister Agda lived on opposite ends of the country. Until the past few years, that had not been a problem. But as their mother grew older, so did the level of Dominic's concern for her. However, at eighty-one Marta Markos was still very independent, and she wanted to stay that way for as long as she could manage.

Dominic listened to his mother's story about the women with whom she volunteered at their local church. His mother, along with a small group of volunteers, provided baby clothes, diapers, and other supplies to mothers in need. Recently, the local news ran a story about the group of volunteers and the good they were doing in the community. As a result of the exposure, donations had begun to pour in, keeping the volunteers busier than ever.

Sitting at his desk, Dominic continued to multitask as his mother wrapped up her story. "So, what about you, Dom? You're not working too hard, are you? Seems like every time I call you're at the restaurant. When do you have time for yourself? You work so hard. When was the last time you went out with friends?"

Dominic smiled. "Friends" was his mother's euphemism for "girlfriend." Marta didn't like that her son had no one to come home to or to take care of him. She conveniently ignored the fact that at forty-seven he was fully capable of taking care of himself and had been doing so for many years.

"Mom, you know how much I love the restaurant, and I'm here because this is my business and it's where I need to be. Preparing good food, spending time with my customers, and making people happy makes me happy too." He thought about the comments he heard from customers when he occasionally walked through the dining room to greet customers. One customer in particular flashed through his mind. Remembering his brief interaction with Ilsa brought another smile to his face.

Dominic heard his mother exhale, bringing him back to the present conversation. She sounded tired.

"Mom, I want you to give some serious thought to coming out for a visit. Then you can see for yourself that I'm fine. Plus, I'll get the chance to pamper you for a change."

Marta laughed. Her son's idea of pampering wasn't quite the same as hers. He meant well though, and she appreciated the sentiment nonetheless.

"So, what do you say? Maybe sometime in the next few months? Plan to stay for a while. You know how you love the beautiful colors of fall. That might be a good time. It probably won't be cold that early, and the leaves should be ready to turn."

Before she could answer, Marta heard her son's muffled voice and instinctively knew he was needed.

"Sorry, Mom. I've got to run. Let's continue this conversation later. In the meantime, I'll take a look at flights for late September. I love you."

Marta barely got out "I love you" before the line went dead.

In just a matter of minutes, Dominic was caught up in one situation after another. Before he had a chance to catch his breath, the lunchtime rush was in full swing, followed by a private company event that segued right into the dinner rush.

It was well after nine o'clock that evening before Dominic had a chance to get back to his office. It had been a long and extremely busy day, something he didn't mind one bit. Making delectable culinary dishes, creating a welcoming atmosphere, and seeing his customers enjoying themselves was something he never grew tired of. But he also knew that he had to take care of himself and not let the restaurant consume him, as his mother often warned.

Running his hand through his hair, he was reminded that it was past time for a haircut. Other than going to the gym, he had been neglecting himself and a few other responsibilities lately. His car needed an oil change, his dry cleaning had piled up, and he hadn't been on a date in ages. Afraid his mother might be right, he put a reminder in his phone to schedule a haircut and get an oil change on Monday. Moving the mouse to awaken his computer, he was interrupted by his cell phone vibrating before he had a chance to check his email. Because of the noise level in the kitchen and his desire to avoid disturbing patrons in the dining room, he typically kept the ringer off and vibrate on.

The number on the caller display wasn't familiar to him, but he answered anyway.

"Hello, this is Dominic," he said in a tone he reserved for strangers.

"Um...hi," said the hesitant voice on the other end. "This is Ilsa. Ilsa Tanner. We met at your restaurant the other day."

Dominic sat up a little straighter, forgetting all about haircuts, oil changes, or that he was supposed to be checking email.

"Of course I remember you." He didn't think he'd ever forget her. "I was beginning to wonder if you were ever going to call."

Ilsa sat up in her bed, setting aside the files she had been working on. She tried to think of something clever to say, but nothing came to mind. Denita, who had advised her to keep the conversation light and sexy, would be so disappointed if she knew how pathetic this was going.

"To be honest, I was seriously deliberating if I would or not."

"Really?" Dominic asked, trying to hide his excitement. "So what was the deciding factor?"

"A quarter."

"A what?"

"You know, a coin."

"As in you flipped a coin?"

"Actually, yes."

Dominic leaned back in his chair and laughed.

Ilsa smiled. Forgetting all about trying to sound cute and sexy, she decided instead to be honest and hoped he wouldn't be offended that she had left the possibility of the two of them ever connecting to a coin toss. At least she made him laugh—a deep, sexy sound which she found that she liked very much.

"So tell me, what would it take for me to see you again? A Magic 8 ball? Tarot cards?"

This time it was Ilsa who laughed out loud. A sense of humor. She liked that. "No. You only have to ask."

"Well, then, I'm asking," he said.

"And I'm accepting."

CHAPTER FOUR

Ilsa scanned the paperwork for the partnership New Hope wanted to form with the city's free health clinic. The partnership would allow their clients to receive free or low-cost health care for themselves and their dependents. She wanted to make sure all the details were worked out before sending it to Grant who, despite the fact she had been developing these types of partnerships for years, felt the need to oversee practically everything she did.

She was writing a clarification in the margin of a copy of the document when she heard someone tapping on her office door. Priscilla stepped in with a small stack of papers.

"What's this?" Ilsa asked.

"Grant wants you to review these invoices."

Ilsa flipped through the first five invoices in the stack and stopped, glancing up at her admin with a look of concern and frustration. "Does he realize these expenses have already been approved? They just need to be sent to accounting to be paid."

Priscilla took a seat across from her boss. "That's exactly what I told him."

"And?"

"And he said he wants you to *re-evaluate the money* that is being spent and to see if there is any way we can be more *prudent* with our funds."

Priscilla was using so many air quotes Ilsa didn't know what words Grant had actually used.

"If you ask me, hiring that man was a big mistake," Priscilla remarked. "He doesn't understand *anything*."

Ilsa placed the stack of invoices off to the side of her desk. Grant had already gone for the day, which wasn't unusual for him. He typically came in late and left early while requiring everyone else to do the opposite. She hid her frustration as best as she could, but she would definitely have to talk to him about the invoices on Monday. Besides, she'd had enough for one week. Friday at five o'clock would be where she'd leave this matter for now.

"It'll be fine, Priscilla. Don't worry about it. I'll work this out with Grant on Monday."

Ilsa began shutting down her computer and gathering her things so she could finally go home and unwind. "Go home and enjoy your weekend," she ordered. "I think we've both had enough."

Priscilla didn't need to be told twice. She hurried out to her desk and grabbed her things.

As they rode the elevator down, Priscilla reminded Ilsa about the reports that would be needed for an upcoming meeting. However, before she had a chance to grimace about the time and effort it would take to pull the reports together, in addition to the other documentation Grant insisted was also needed, a muffled ringing came from her bag. Ilsa fumbled around inside her bag, found her phone, and answered the call before it went to voice mail.

"Hello, Ilsa Tanner. I have an offer I hope you can't refuse."

Dominic.

Smiling, Ilsa replied. "Well, that's a loaded sentence."

Priscilla noticed the huge smile on her boss' face but unfortunately had to be across town to pick up her kids from daycare and didn't have time to eavesdrop or pry for details. Priscilla shot Ilsa a knowing look and a wink before she headed to her car, letting her know she expected details on Monday.

"Are you still at work?"

"Just leaving."

"Perfect. I'm leaving the restaurant too."

"On a Friday night? Isn't that like primetime in the restaurant business?"

Dominic didn't share the details about everything he had put in place so he could have the night off in hopes of spending some time with her. Regardless of the effort, he knew it would be worth it.

"No, everything is covered. They don't need me," he said, trying to sound unconcerned. "Are you near downtown?"

"Sort of. Did you want me to meet you somewhere tonight? I thought we were meeting for brunch on Sunday."

"Yes, I do and, yes, Sunday is still on. I just wanted to see you before then...if you're free." Dominic grimaced and cautioned himself to slow down. The last thing he wanted was for Ilsa to think he was being pushy, but he did want to see her and Sunday wasn't soon enough.

Just minutes earlier, the only thing Ilsa had wanted was to go home, turn off her brain, and veg in front of the TV. But since Dominic offered something that might be more appealing, she rethought her previous plans.

"Can you meet me in thirty minutes downtown at Goodale Park?"

Ilsa checked her watch, wondering if she had time to go home and freshen up. Factoring in rush hour traffic and the amount of construction occurring along practically every route she needed to take, there was no way she could make it home and back in under thirty minutes.

"I'm still wearing my work clothes if that's okay."

"I'm sure whatever you're wearing will be fine. I promise we won't be hiking or anything like that."

Before pulling out of the parking lot, Ilsa sat in her car scrounging around inside her extra-large and overstuffed bag, hoping to find some lipstick and eyeliner. She was going to have to use some makeup magic to look as presentable as possible and not like someone who had been putting out small fires all day at work.

Dominic pulled his car into a spot on the street adjacent to the park. He had arrived early on purpose. Looking around, he didn't see Ilsa. Not knowing the kind of car she drove, he'd have to wait for her to get out and look for him once she arrived.

He grabbed some things from his car along with a large blanket from the trunk. Surveying the park grounds, he looked around for just the right spot. For the most part, the park wasn't very busy at all, which was ideal. This was one of the nicer and most accessible parks; it could easily be crowded and not conducive to what he had in mind—a quiet but public place to spend some time with Ilsa.

Walking up a small hill, he scoped out a spot he thought was perfect. A small group of kids was playing soccer nearby, but they wouldn't be close enough to bother them. A few families and couples were also out enjoying the park in what could be described as the perfect summer evening.

Dominic spread out the blanket he had brought from the car, leaned against a tree, and waited patiently for her to arrive.

Ilsa sat in what had to be the slowest-moving traffic ever. Surrounded by orange barrels, construction workers, and loud machines, she scolded herself for not avoiding this particular route. She had planned to arrive at the park before Dominic and to appear calm, cool, and as unbothered as possible. Now she would be showing up late, flustered, and apologetic.

"Ugh! Move it, people," she said aloud, although no one could hear her outside of her car.

Finally, there was a break in traffic. She cut around to a side street, taking the scenic, albeit faster, route to the park. When she finally arrived, she waited before getting out of the car. She hated being late, particularly this time. Oddly, she didn't want to make a bad impression.

She stepped out and looked around for Dominic. He had told her to meet him on the south end of the park, but she didn't see him. His only other instruction was to meet him at the park in thirty minutes. She wasn't sure what he had in mind, but the spontaneity of the whole thing appealed to her.

"Ilsa."

Turning in the direction of the voice that was becoming increasingly familiar, she smiled when she saw Dominic standing under a large shade tree waving to her. As she approached, a large blanket spread out on the ground and what appeared to be a wicker picnic basket caught her attention.

"Hi," he said, greeting her with an unexpected kiss on the cheek and quick hug.

"Hi." She tried not to smile too broadly. He was tall, she noted. In addition to his good looks, that was a bonus. She liked tall men. For some reason she hadn't picked up on that before; maybe because she'd been seated and preoccupied, checking out his other features.

At five-eight, she often felt as if she towered over most men, especially when she wore heels. With Dominic, that wouldn't be a problem.

Dominic looked nice. He was casually dressed, not sloppy or like he didn't care. His black linen pants were topped with a light green shirt that gave his skin a bronze glow. She wondered if he was this tan all the time or if his skin had been bronzed from spending time in the summer sun.

His thick, black hair was cut close on the sides, a little longer on top, and curling up just a bit on the ends. Seeing how good he looked, she immediately regretted not having moved their meeting out thirty to forty-five minutes more so she would have had a chance to change clothes and spruce herself up a bit. Eyeliner and lipstick could only do so much.

"You look beautiful," he said, smiling down at her.

Self-consciously running her hand over her natural curls and thankful her twist out actually turned out the way she had intended, she thanked him. The next time he saw her she would be more put together, she secretly vowed.

Dominic motioned for her to take a seat on the blanket.

Sitting down and getting into a comfortable position she started to apologize. "I'm sorry for being late. Traffic on High Street was a mess, and I got caught in the middle of all the construction chaos."

Dominic sat across from her and shrugged. "It's okay. You're worth the wait."

Flattered and a little amused, she asked playfully, "What makes you so sure?"

"Call it instinct," he said.

Lowering heavily lashed eyes, Dominic smiled. *This woman.* She made him feel, say, and do things that weren't typical for him. If he wasn't careful he would end up letting it slip how much he had been thinking about her all day, actually since the moment they'd met. They'd only had two brief interactions—once in person and once over the phone—but each time had been memorable. The sound of her voice, the way she laughed, and how incredibly beautiful he found her to be seemed to constantly occupy his conscious and unconscious thoughts.

His smile. Ilsa's tummy did a little dip. The way he smiled at her just then—kind of devilish and a little mischievous—elevated him from attractive in the looks department to flat-out *wow*. And damn if that five o'clock shadow wasn't the cherry on top!

Usually, she was pretty good at assessing people but was unsure about the vibe she was getting from Dominic. On one hand, he was obviously flirting—the smile, how he looked at her, and the way he seemed to study her face, coupled with the kiss on the cheek and the hug. But, on the other hand, he seemed to be holding back a little, choosing his words carefully. Maybe he was holding back because they didn't know each other that well and he didn't want to be too aggressive. Or maybe he was nervous. Funny, she couldn't remember the last time she had made a man nervous. The thought was flattering and gave her a little ego boost. Maybe she still had *it* after all this time.

"So, Dominic Markos, what do you have planned for us this evening? I'm intrigued by the picnic basket."

What did he have planned? Dominic had to be careful about what he said next. He wanted so badly to make a good impression, and the last thing he wanted was to say or do the wrong thing. So far things appeared to be going well, and she liked the idea of having a picnic, but he was still trying to calm his nerves.

From the moment he spotted her stepping out of her car, his heart began to race. He wanted to tell her how happy he was that she had accepted his invitation. But he didn't. He had to play it cool. But when he hugged her, he hadn't expected to feel what he felt—something he couldn't accurately describe. It was a connection, a feeling, a vibe. Had she felt it too?

They were essentially strangers, and he didn't want to move too fast. He needed to keep a cool head, but she didn't make it easy.

Ilsa had mentioned over the phone that she was wearing her "work clothes." At the time he couldn't picture what that meant. But when he saw her he was more than pleased; she looked perfect. Wearing a simple pair of pants that showed off a slim waist and curvy hips paired with a silky peach sleeveless top that moved effortlessly with her body and complimented her deep brown skin, he had to busy his hands to keep from reaching out and running his fingertips down her arms, feeling what he knew was smooth, soft skin. To further weaken his resolve, whatever scent she was wearing practically made his mouth water. Not to mention the touch of color that accented her beautiful lips made him wonder what kissing her would be like. He didn't know how to explain the sudden urge to kiss her, and it surprised him.

A little breeze kicked up, tossing her curls about. Something else he'd noticed when he first spotted her at the restaurant: her hair—curly, big, and free. Although tempted, he knew better than to touch her hair. But sooner or later she was going to have to let him get his fingers tangled in her coiled tresses.

Clearing his throat and calming racing thoughts, Dominic brought the picnic basket closer to him.

"Well, I have a picnic planned for us. Hungry?"

"Starving."

He began unpacking the basket, pulling out container after container until Ilsa, hungry and impressed, asked, "When did you have time to do all this?"

Her enthusiasm pleased him. "That's a perk of owning a restaurant."

Dominic passed Ilsa a napkin, plate, and eating utensils. "Have you ever had fennel?"

"Cooked, but I've never tried it raw. Since I'm pretty hungry, I'm willing to try everything," she replied, eyeing the mini feast spread out in front of her.

Taking a bite of fennel along with a chunk of thick, crusty bread wrapped in prosciutto, she closed her eyes and sighed. "This is absolutely delicious."

"If you like that, then you're going to love this."

Ilsa eyed the colorful concoction he scooped on her plate.

Dominic watched as she sampled a forkful. He didn't have to ask if she liked it or not. She immediately repeated the same closed eyes and sighing thing.

"Antipasti," he replied to the raised eyebrow and unasked question.

Pleased, Dominic popped an olive in his mouth and fixed himself a plate. Between bites and casual conversation about food, he watched as Ilsa ate everything he put on her plate.

"That," she said, dabbing the corners of her mouth with her napkin, "was beyond words."

Dominic was beside himself, pleased with his picnic idea and the foods he'd chosen. He loved watching her eat. He could tell she enjoyed the food, taking her time sampling everything and not rushing. There was a kind of sensual element to the whole thing. He hated when women picked over their plates, never eating anything, just moving the food around as if they had eaten. And he could not stand picky eaters or people unwilling to try new tastes and textures.

"Did you prepare this whole meal yourself?"

He nodded. "I have a very skilled chef who could have done just as good a job, but I wanted to impress you," he admitted.

Again, flattered by this man, Ilsa smiled. "Mission accomplished."

"So, Ilsa Tanner, now that you've had a satisfying meal, not to mention the outstanding service, it's time for you to do something for me."

Eyeing him suspiciously, she asked, "What's that?" *Is this it*, she wondered. *Is this where he shows his crazy?* Unconsciously, she looked at her purse, wondering if she'd have to use her pepper spray.

"Tell me about yourself."

Relieved that he hadn't turned into some weirdo or wanted her to do something completely insane, she relaxed.

"Well, I'm a native Buckeye, born and raised outside of Cincinnati."

"What brought you to Columbus?"

"My husband. After we got married his job transferred him here."

Married? Dominic was caught off guard. He had already checked for a wedding ring back at the restaurant when they first met and again today. So he was pretty sure, at least he hoped, she wasn't married. He noticed that she never once said "ex-husband."

"Your husband..."

"Passed away several years ago," she finished.

"I'm sorry," he replied sincerely.

Ilsa's smile was a little sad as she continued. "It's okay. What doesn't kill you makes you stronger, right?"

Dominic nodded but was at a loss for what to say next.

In an attempt to lighten the mood she told him about her sons. "I also have a new daughter-in-law. My youngest son recently got married."

"Congratulations."

"Thanks. I'm still trying to get used to that."

"So what do you do for a living?"

"I'm the associate director of a non-profit agency, New Hope Family Center. We provide services—job placement assistance, transportation, and help with affordable and safe housing—to women in need."

"Hmm...that seems to fit your personality."

"What about you? I know you own YiaYia's Table and can pull together a mean picnic. What else?"

Dominic leaned back on his elbows and thought for a second. "Well, I'm also an Ohio native, born and raised in Columbus, not too far from here. That's why I invited you to meet me at this park. It's one of my favorite places. My sister and I spent a lot of time playing here when we were kids."

"Do you have kids?"

He shook his head. "I was married, briefly, a long time ago. We were both way too young to know what we were doing, and the marriage suffered. I think we were more in lust than in love. Anyway, we never had kids."

"Parents?"

"My father died several years back."

"I'm sorry."

Dominic nodded and thought briefly about his father. He would have liked Ilsa. Although he had been true to his wife and loved her dearly, Dominic's father had been a big flirt and had a thing for pretty women.

"After my father died and my mother retired, she moved to Arizona, unlike a lot of her friends who relocated to Florida. She said she didn't like Florida—too many old people."

They both laughed.

"Pet peeves?"

Amused with the game of rapid-fire questions, Dominic continued to play along. "Let's see...people who know *everything* and refuse to listen to anyone else's opinion."

"I'm completely with you on that. So just the one sister?"

"Yes. She's the youngest."

"Big brother. Okay. Possible bully. I'll tuck that nugget of information away for later," she joked. "Favorite movie?"

"Well, I'm half Italian, so it would be a crime if I didn't list at least one *Rocky* movie. But because they were all masterpieces, I'm going to have to include the entire franchise."

"Italian, huh," Ilsa remarked more to herself than Dominic.

"And Greek. My mother is Italian and my father was Greek."

"Interesting."

"My turn."

"Fair enough. Go."

"Favorite meal?"

"Besides this one?" she asked, pointing to the remnants of their picnic. "I'd have to say a cheeseburger with extra sharp cheddar, dill pickle wedge, french fries, and a thick chocolate milkshake."

"Very Midwestern and a good choice. What about siblings?"

"Two sisters. One older, one younger, still living in the Cincinnati area."

"Interesting. Middle child. I'll have to remember that."

Wrinkling her brow, she asked, "What's that supposed to mean?"

Dominic wagged a finger. "It's my turn to ask questions, remember?"

Ilsa tossed her napkin at him and he ducked.

"Next question. Favorite movie?"

"Let's see, that's kind of tough. I actually have more than one, but I'll share my top three. *Night of the Living Dead*, the black and white version, *Aliens*, and *To Sir with Love*, in no particular order."

Ilsa laughed when she saw the mock horror-stricken look on Dominic's face.

"I know. An amazing list of cinematic delights," she replied.

Dominic shook his head in disbelief. "I'm almost afraid to ask what other movies you have on your list."

"It's a most impressive list, and definitely not for the faint of heart. Play your cards right, and I might share it with you one day."

"I'm sure I'll be entertained if not scarred for life. Okay, one more question. What is that perfume you're wearing?"

"Do you like it?" she asked, wracking her brain trying to remember that morning's combination of scents.

Dominic raised his eyebrows. "Very much. I don't usually pay attention to stuff like that, and I don't know any other way to say this, but you smell nice."

"To be honest, I don't remember everything I used this morning."

"Everything?"

"Yeah, I like to experiment with different fragrances. I typically mix different scented oils and lotions until I come up with something that matches my mood, the occasion, or the weather. For example, on rainy days, I like something light and earthy. When it's hot, I like fresh, citrusy, or floral scents."

Wondering if her explanation sounded a little odd, she saw him smile and got the impression he understood the method to her madness.

Again that smile. It was starting to grow on her.

"Does that sound weird?"

"Not at all. I knew you were different—in a good way—the first time I saw you," he said, sounding more serious than he intended. "One more question."

"You said that one question ago."

"But this one is important."

"Okay, I'll grant you one more," she teased.

Smiling, Dominic sat up, looked into her eyes, and asked, "Will you dance with me?"

CHAPTER FIVE

"Hey, don't be selfish. You need to share. I would love to have some of your happy juice."

Dominic was only half paying attention. "Happy juice?"

"No one is this happy at ten in the morning without a little extra *oomph* in their coffee."

"What? There's nothing in here but coffee," Dominic replied, holding his cup up for inspection.

Lu, the restaurant's general manager, part-time bartender, marketing guru, and webmistress—or, as Dominic often called her, "the hardest working woman in the restaurant business"—stood in front of his desk peering down with an amused look on her face.

"Well, whatever it is, I want some of the magic elixir that's put you in such a good mood."

Dominic looked over the sample postcard Lu had created for an upcoming promotion, carefully reading the front and back before nodding his approval. "I don't know what you're talking about. I'm always in a good mood. And these look great. Let's start the email campaign, and get these out to everyone who dines in as soon as possible."

Lu sat on the corner of Dominic's desk, picked up his coffee cup, and took a sip. She made a face. "What do you know? It actually is coffee. But seriously, I don't know how you can stand to drink it black though. Ugh!"

"Get out, Lu. Go make yourself useful," he playfully ordered.

"I'm the most useful person around this place. You'd better be nice to me," she said on her way out of the office.

She was right. Dominic had lucked out when he hired Lu. She came with a wealth of restaurant, customer service, and computer experience. Plus, she designed all of the restaurant's promotional material and kept their website and social media pages up to date. The woman was a dynamo, and he made sure to keep her happy.

He respected and appreciated Lu and gave her free creative rein over many aspects of managing the restaurant. In turn, she worked hard and was fiercely loyal. Before the restaurant opened and the months that followed the opening, the two of them had worked a lot of late nights and early mornings together. At times it seemed as if she had as much passion for his dream as he did. Over time their work relationship had turned into a comfortable brother/annoying little sister type of bond. They often shared things that were going on in their lives but respected the unspoken boundaries of boss and employee. He wondered if he should tell her about meeting Ilsa. If things worked out, the two of them would inevitably meet when he bought Ilsa to the restaurant.

Over the years Dominic hadn't dated much. After leaving his corporate job and opening the restaurant he simply did not have the time or patience needed for a relationship. Truth be told, he had not met anyone interesting enough to put forth the time or effort. Sure, he met his share of women through the restaurant, but casual relationships weren't his thing, and most women didn't want to put up with the odd hours he was required to work to keep his business afloat.

But there was something about Ilsa that made him eager to put forth an effort. He felt even more strongly about that after the time they'd spent together the previous day.

The picnic and then dancing after—he leaned his elbows on the desk and stared off into the distance. He couldn't remember the last time he had enjoyed himself that much. Thankfully, his nerves had calmed down enough that he stopped worrying about saying or doing the wrong thing. The more time he spent with Ilsa, the more comfortable in her presence he became.

The picnic had been something impromptu that had come to him while he was sitting in this very spot, thinking about Ilsa. He had wanted to see her; even though they were planning to meet for brunch on Sunday, he wanted to see her before then.

By the time he called that evening, he had already prepared everything for their outing, stepping out on faith. He smiled. He'd actually been nervous dialing her number, secretly praying that she didn't already have plans. It was a good thing that she hadn't been able to see his face when she agreed to meet him because he had been grinning from ear to ear.

The picnic had turned out better than he expected. Not knowing what foods she liked, he had chosen several tried-and-true options that most anyone would have enjoyed. And she had. She genuinely liked the food he brought, and he enjoyed watching her as she tried a little of everything. Again, there was something to be said about a person who takes the time to enjoy their food.

As the picnic was coming to an end, he found himself searching for something else to do, anything that would allow him to spend more time with her. He wasn't ready for their time together to end. Then he remembered a place Lu had told him about that was not too far from the park that offered salsa lessons on Friday nights and later opened up to dancing once the class ended. He wasn't sure if Ilsa would be interested, but when he made the suggestion, she readily accepted.

During the lesson, the two of them laughed as they fumbled learning the *bachata* after easily picking up the techniques for *salsa* and *meringue*. The only thing Dominic didn't like was the requirement to frequently change partners while learning each dance. But once the class ended and the place opened up for everyone to dance—for those who had taken lessons and those who just wanted to come and dance—that's when he could dance with Ilsa exclusively.

The two of them swayed to the lively Latin and Caribbean music, and he even remembered enough of the *meringue* to attempt making a few turns. Although at one point, during a turn, something went wrong—or right in his opinion—and Ilsa landed back in his arms, standing face to face, bodies pressed together.

She felt good in his arms, and she looked so sexy when she was dancing. The instructor had stressed the importance of moving one's hips when dancing, and Ilsa had followed his instructions to a T. The way she moved her hips, swayed her shoulders, and allowed the music to take over her body made him forget anyone else was in the room. He loved dancing with her and watching her dance. This was definitely something they would have to do again.

Yesterday Lu hadn't questioned him when he asked her to run things while he was gone, but he knew it was just a matter of time before he would have to let her know what was going on. He couldn't keep Ilsa to himself much longer. He had a feeling his heart wouldn't allow it.

CHAPTER SIX

Awakened by the incessant ringing of her phone, Ilsa fumbled to pick it up from her nightstand and answer before the call rolled to voicemail. Turning over on her back, she willed herself to wake up enough to speak. "Hello?" she croaked out, voice groggy, head foggy.

"Where have you been?"

"What?"

"I tried calling you at least three times last night, and I sent you no less than four text messages."

Blinking and trying to adjust to the bright sunlight streaming in her room, Ilsa let her head rest against her pillow and yawned.

"Are you all right?" Denita's concern was evident and immediate. "Is something going on? Do I need to come over?"

Ilsa covered her tired eyes with her one free hand and giggled, remembering why she was so tired. "No, Denita, I'm fine. Nothing is going on other than sleep."

"Something's not right. It's almost ten o'clock, and it's obvious you're still in bed. Are you sure I don't need to come over? And what are you giggling about?"

Hearing the concern in her friend's voice made her feel a little guilty. Realizing she had left her phone in the bottom of her bag in the trunk of her car while she went dancing with Dominic, she knew she'd have to come up with a good excuse to give Denita for basically throwing caution to the wind and being completely unreachable. To make matters worse, she hadn't even seen the messages or missed calls until she'd arrived home; by that time, it had been much too late to return the calls.

"I'm sorry, but I'm laughing at you, Mother Hen."

True, Denita could be quite protective but only because she truly cared about Ilsa and wanted her to be happy. Denita kept a close circle of friends amongst her many acquaintances. And if one found themselves in that small circle, they should count themselves blessed. Denita Harper was a true friend, in every sense of the word.

"Now, going back to my original question, where have you been?"

The memory of her time spent with Dominic brought a quick and very broad smile to Ilsa's face. This time she tried very hard to suppress a giggle. She momentarily debated on how much she should tell Denita but then decided to tell her everything. She owed her an explanation, and there was no real reason to leave anything out.

"I was with Dominic."

Ilsa heard a slight gasp.

"Do you mean that fine man from the restaurant? The one who couldn't take his eyes off you and the one I insisted you call?" she added in a low, deliberate tone.

"Yes, ma'am." She purposely ignored her friend's sarcasm.

"Oh, my...details! Wait. First, need I remind you that you're supposed to call, text, fax, or send by carrier pigeon any and all communication about a first date? There are too many nut jobs out there, and you're supposed to let someone—namely me—know where you are and who you're with just in case I have to show up and show out."

"Yes, Mother."

"Okay, now I want details."

"When I was leaving work last night, I got a call with an invitation to meet at a park."

"A park?"

"Mm-hmm. There were no other instructions except where to park my car. So in the spirit of spontaneity, something you keep encouraging me to be, I said yes and I met Dominic at Goodale Park. Denita, let me tell you, this man had a picnic dinner all set up when I got there, complete with the picnic basket, blanket, and the most delicious meal I've had in a long time."

"Sounds like he put a lot of time and effort into this *impromptu* date."

"He said he didn't, but it doesn't matter because we had a lot of fun. We talked, ate, and laughed and got to know each other a little better."

"And?"

"And he's funny and smart and a lot of fun. We even went dancing after the picnic."

"Dancing? So were you trying to make up in one night for years of not being spontaneous?"

"Haha. No, smarty. He suggested it. I thought it sounded like fun and I said yes."

"Is he a good dancer?"

Ilsa reflected on their dance lessons and how quickly Dominic picked up most of the steps. She liked dancing with him. He had a gentle way of holding her when they danced to the slower songs. During the faster songs, he never missed a beat, except during one song when they were supposed to do a series of steps and then a turn.

Somehow their steps were off, and the turn was even more off, causing Ilsa to land back in Dominic's arms, bodies pressed against each other much closer than she had expected. Even though their dance steps were off, it felt pretty nice. They had definitely shared a moment.

"Yes, very."

"Anything after dancing? Maybe a midnight rendezvous somewhere?"

"No. Nothing like that, although we did talk on the ride home. He wanted to make sure I made it home safely. But the funny thing is, when I got home we still kept talking. I think he didn't want to get off the phone." *And neither did I.* "Felt like tenth grade and a first crush all over again, but very grown-up."

"So what's next?"

"What do you mean?" Ilsa didn't even try to stifle a yawn.

"Any other dates lined up?"

She hadn't told Denita about her plans to meet Dominic for brunch on Sunday. She wasn't sure why. She just hadn't.

"Yes, we're meeting for brunch tomorrow."

"Is he cooking?"

"I don't know. He's coming by to pick me up, and he didn't say where we were going."

Satisfied that her friend was okay and growing tired of hearing her yawning, she decided to let her go. "Well, have fun. Don't do anything I wouldn't do, but if you do, tell me all about it."

Disconnecting the call, Ilsa rolled over in bed and groaned. She had things to do and needed to get out of bed. As much as she'd like to, she couldn't lie around all day doing nothing.

After she showered and got dressed, Ilsa sat down to breakfast and decided to log on and check her work email. The first thing she noticed was an email from Grant. Slamming her cup down and spilling coffee on the table, Ilsa swore. The new computer equipment they were supposed to receive in the fall was just put on hold so Grant could "evaluate the need for the expenditure." The center's staff had been promised that equipment for nearly two years; now, in one uninformed and rash decision, that would no longer be happening.

"What is wrong with him?" she said aloud in her empty kitchen. The man was micromanaging and re-evaluating practically every decision she and the staff made, for no apparent reason other than he could. She didn't know who he was trying to impress or what he hoped to accomplish, but she hoped it happened soon so he could stop getting in the way of progress.

After almost a year, she was nearing the end of her patience with Grant.

Ilsa cleaned up the spilled coffee and shut down her computer. Grant was going to be a problem. She had given him a year to change, and he had only gotten worse. It was time to form a plan to keep him from causing any more damage. The health and welfare of those who depended on the services of New Hope depended on it. Too much good work had been done over the years, and there was still a lot left to do. She refused to let some micromanaging, corporate reject ruin any of that.

CHAPTER SEVEN

Ilsa came home after church to tidy up a bit. Dominic told her he would be by around one to pick her up, and she wanted to be ready. They hadn't talked since their marathon phone conversation following their drive home Friday night. The conversation had lasted well into the wee hours of the morning, but she hadn't minded one bit. Instead of a follow-up phone call, she had received a few text messages from Dominic on Saturday. The restaurant had been very busy, but he had taken quick breaks here and there to let her know he was thinking about her and couldn't wait to see her again.

Ilsa picked up her cell phone from the coffee table. She found Dominic's messages and read them again. Smiling, she sat down on the sofa while she waited.

She liked Dominic, and she liked spending time with him. He was funny and smart and very sweet. Being with him felt good and, so far, didn't require her to be "on." She felt she could be herself around him with no pretenses. A few of the men she had dated over the years had wanted very specific qualities in a woman, from dressing a certain way to driving a particular kind of car or even being the "right" size. These days she didn't have the temperament to deal with any of that. *Take me or leave me. Just don't try to change me.*

There were many things she was discovering she liked about Dominic, but one thing in particular she noticed was that he paid attention to little things. When they were talking Friday night/Saturday morning, he had asked her something about her daughter-in-law and had even remembered her name and the names of her sons.

Dominic had also been very attentive when they were on their picnic. He watched for her reactions as she tried the different foods. The attention made her a little nervous at first, especially since she had gobbled down everything he'd put on her plate. But she didn't think he cared about her appetite, only that she was enjoying herself.

She leaned back on the sofa and recalled how quickly she had accepted Dominic's invitation to go dancing. Other than in her Zumba class, she hadn't danced in years, but the idea had sounded interesting.

Still smiling, she also recalled the look on Dominic's face when the dance instructor told them about the requirement that the men take a step to their left to a new partner with the instruction and practice of each new step. Dominic had grabbed her hand and said to the instructor, "I don't want to switch partners. I want to dance with her." To which the instructor replied, "You will, once I teach you how to stay off her toes."

Snapped back to the present by her phone signaling that she had a new email, Ilsa checked and saw it was nothing she needed to pay attention to at the moment.

Twelve fifty-five.

Checking her reflection in the mirror once more, she was pretty satisfied with what she saw. She had debated over whether to wear her hair up in a puff with spiraled curls or down and free. She chose down and free. She thought Dominic might like it that way. When they were together at the park, she thought she had caught him looking at her hair a few times. He'd even remarked how much he liked how she styled it. Ever since she began styling and wearing her hair in its natural state, she would often receive comments or questions from perfect strangers. "Is that your *real* hair?" "How do you get your hair like that?" "Can I touch it?" *Seriously, who asks can they touch a stranger's hair?*

Ding dong.

Ilsa took in a deep breath and slowly let it out. Not wanting to appear too eager, she waited a few seconds before answering the door with a smile.

"Hi." She motioned for Dominic to come inside.

"Hi." He stepped in and greeted her with a hug and kiss on the cheek.

She was beginning to like that, this little show of affection.

"Don't you look pretty." He reached out and gingerly pulled and released one of her curls.

Taken aback, Ilsa frowned. *He did not just...*

The look on Ilsa's face did not go unnoticed. "I'm sorry," he said with a devilish grin. "Don't be upset. I've been dying to do that since Friday. Your hair is beautiful and I love it. I couldn't resist touching it just once."

His smile had an instant effect on her. How could she be mad, especially with him wearing that sexy grin? It was a forgivable offense.

"Ready?"

She quickly regained her composure. Grabbing her purse and flinging it on her shoulder, she turned and announced, "I am now."

Walking out the front door and around to her driveway, Ilsa started to ask where they were going for brunch but stopped dead in her tracks when she saw what was parked in the driveway.

"Is this yours? That's a '69 Chevy Camaro," she exclaimed before Dominic could answer. Taking a few tentative steps toward the beautiful machine, she quietly *oohed* and *ahhed*. Surprised and excited, she added almost breathlessly, "An SS. You weren't driving this when we met at the park, were you? I would have noticed this car parked on the street. She is yours, right?"

Dominic was surprised too. "Yes, she's mine, but I only drive her sometimes." He didn't know why he was suddenly feminizing his car since he had never done it before. Now, he felt like he was supposed to. "I wasn't driving her the other day. Wait, you know about cars?"

She nodded and walked around the body of the freshly detailed car. "Not all cars, but this kind of car, yes." She bent down and looked at the tires. "My dad had one of these when I was a little girl. He would spend hours in the garage working on Belle, his name for the car. When he first got her, she was a little more than a rusty, neglected heap."

He watched as she walked around the car with open admiration. When she made it back to the passenger's side, Dominic opened the door so she could get in, but he didn't step aside. Instead, he grabbed her shoulders, pulling her into him as his lips came down on hers.

Surprised but not displeased, Ilsa momentarily forgot all about the car, focusing only on the fact that Dominic was kissing her and she was enjoying every second of it. Warm, sensual, and sexy, she instantly blocked out everything but this man who had removed all space separating them and seemed to have caused time to stop. *Was she even breathing? Did she need to?*

"That," he said breathlessly when the kiss ended, "was for being sexy *and* amazing."

Ilsa smiled and touched her lips as she took her seat and waited for him to join her in the car. *What just happened?* Her heart pounded and her breathing came in quick, short puffs of air.

Dominic walked around the car as his heart raced. *What just happened?* Their first kiss. Wow! It was everything he thought it would be and more, even though he hadn't expected it to happen at that moment. Something came over him, and this time he couldn't stop himself—nor did he want to.

Dominic sat in the driver's seat. Hesitating before he started the ignition, he turned to Ilsa. "That kiss, it was nice. I hope we can share more of those."

"Most definitely," she responded.

Ilsa smiled as a million tingles raced through her body. She could have easily rationalized her feelings, attributing her reaction to the thrill of being in this magnificent car, but she knew better. It was the thrill of being with the man sitting next to her.

As the Camaro's engine roared to life, Ilsa's smile broadened. "This brings back so many memories. When I was younger I loved spending time hanging out with my dad. It didn't matter what he was doing. I especially loved hanging out in our old garage when he was working on Belle. Back then I was sort of a daddy's girl."

As they pulled out of the driveway and headed toward their destination, she continued. "My dad doesn't have any sons, and my sisters weren't interested in learning about cars, so he shared what he knew and loved about them with me. I was like a sponge. Everything he wanted to teach me, I was willing to learn. I don't know if it was because I was that interested in cars or more interested in my father's attention."

"Wow," Ilsa whispered when Dominic shifted gears.

"I'm not a *motorhead* like my father, but I think I was a pretty good assistant. He taught me how to change the oil, replace the carburetor, and tune-up Belle."

Listening to Ilsa talk about cars was not only fascinating to Dominic, it was sexy as hell. *This woman!*

Realizing she had been talking the whole time and sure the kiss had something to do with her rapid chattering, she apologized. "I'm sorry. I've been going on and on."

Dominic tried to keep his eyes on the road but couldn't help stealing sideways glances at Ilsa as her excitement spilled over. "I don't mind," he said.

"Good, because I haven't seen one of these in a long time. Did you restore her yourself?"

Dominic nodded. "Me and a buddy of mine. Took us a long time since we only worked on her on the weekends."

"Does she have a name?" she asked tentatively, not wanting to sound silly.

Dominic sensed the hesitation in her voice. He thought the idea of naming his car was cute.

"Good question. I never thought about giving her a proper name. Honestly, before today, I only referred to her as the Camaro. Now I feel neglectful, like I didn't give her the proper respect. Would you like to do the honors?"

Relieved, she accepted the challenge. "Okay, but you do realize this may take some time. I need to get to know her, see what her temperament is like."

"All right. You just let me know when you're ready and we'll make it official."

"How are we going to do that?"

Dominic pulled onto the highway, shifted the car into high gear, and smiled. "That, Ms. Tanner, will be a surprise worth waiting for."

CHAPTER EIGHT

This one hurt. Ilsa stared at the letter of resignation from Brenda, her software installer, spreadsheet expert, and the main person they all relied on to troubleshoot computer and software issues.

Brenda expressed her sadness about having to leave New Hope but said she had found a position with another non-profit agency that happened to be looking for someone with her skills. She also shared privately with Ilsa how much she hated leaving, admitting she could no longer justify staying where she felt her work was not appreciated. Without saying it outright, Ilsa knew her departure centered around Grant and the low morale plaguing New Hope.

Brenda's resignation had been the second one she'd received in three weeks. She tried to remain positive, but losing good people hurt. What bothered her even more was the fact that there wasn't much she could do about it. Doing her best to run interference was no longer enough. Setting boundaries for how he treated her and the staff didn't seem to do much either. She was quickly running out of options for keeping everyone, including herself, sane.

Ilsa stood in the doorway of Grant's office, patiently waiting for him to complete his phone call. She needed to tell him about Brenda.

"Come in," he said when he finished.

"I just received Brenda's letter of resignation."

Grant seemed completely unbothered by the news. "Okay," he replied nonchalantly. "She shouldn't be too hard to replace."

Ilsa couldn't believe what she was hearing. Clearly, he didn't see the downstream effects of Brenda leaving. "I think you're completely undervaluing everything she did around here. We're going to be in a real bind when she leaves. I don't know if you know this, but Brenda has been our go-to person for all things IT. She installs new software, troubleshoots computer issues, trains new staff members, and she's been the key person pulling the statistical data that makes up the reports you've been presenting to the board."

Ilsa believed in cross-training all of her staff members, never wanting to be left in a bind when someone left the agency, taking critical knowledge with them. But in this case, she truly *was* left in a bind. Brenda's back-up had been the person who resigned before her, and Ilsa had yet to replace him.

"Aren't you able to run the reports Brenda produces?"

Reports? Out of everything, that was the one thing he heard? Incredible!

"I can, but Brenda was a whiz at creating queries on the fly. Keep in mind, she did more than run reports."

"Then I suppose you'll need to figure out how she did what she did before she leaves."

Back at her desk Ilsa contemplated how she would handle the sudden staff turnover. Everyone was already taking on extra work and it would continue this way until she filled the open positions. At this point, she simply could not afford to lose any more employees.

Staring at the stack of applications on her desk that had to be reviewed, the phone messages she was supposed to return by the end of the day, and a presentation that needed to be fine-tuned, she couldn't help feeling overwhelmed and unmotivated. Nothing about what she was doing seemed helpful to anyone—not the staff, their clients, or herself. It wasn't like her to view her work at New Hope as just a job, but that was what it was becoming to her.

Resting her head on the back of her chair, she stared at the ceiling. At the moment all she wanted to do was to go home and forget about New Hope, Grant, staffing issues, and anything else threatening to drain her time and energy.

For the most part, she loved her work and in some ways it felt like a calling, but lately she found the passion she once had fading, something she hadn't admitted to anyone and had a hard time admitting to herself.

Sighing wearily, she sat up, willing herself to press on. There didn't seem to be any other option.

Reading through the applications, she reviewed the notes added to each of them from the intake staff. One application caught her attention. The applicant, Tia Phillips, had applied for emergency housing. It was noted on the application that Tia had a job but was only making minimum wage. It appeared that she had been sleeping on friends' couches for the past few weeks after her boyfriend threw her out of his apartment. Now she needed something more permanent. Sadly, Ilsa saw this type of situation more and more. But what caught her attention out of everything was the note from the intake counselor who mentioned Tia's interest in career training.

New Hope had recently partnered with an organization whose mission was to get more women into the technical field—computer coding, graphic design, and systems analysis. Most of the women who had come through their agency weren't even remotely interested in the program, and those who were hadn't met the basic eligibility requirements. This young lady had been flagged as a possible candidate.

Knowing that they had to meet her most immediate housing need first, Ilsa pulled the application and set it aside. She made a few calls and found a bed for her at a women's shelter that was clean, safe, on the bus line, and would allow her to stay until she got on her feet.

Ilsa contacted Tia to tell her about the shelter. She could hear the relief in her voice. After scheduling an appointment for her to come into the office on her day off, Ilsa hung up, relieved that she had started what she hoped would be some positive changes in the young woman's life.

Completing the review of the remaining applications, Ilsa decided to tackle her email. As she read, deleted, or forwarded emails as appropriate, she came to the last email. The subject line read "Thank You," but she didn't recognize the name of the sender.

Opening the email, she read:

"Four years ago my life was a mess and so was I. When I came to New Hope I had just gotten out of jail. I had no place to stay, no money, no support, no job, and no hope. To be honest, I was ready to give up.

A lady I met while I was in jail gave me some information about New Hope and told me to see if they could help me find a place to stay. She was in just as bad shape as I was, but I took her advice with a grain of salt. I showed up for my first appointment not expecting much, and I couldn't have been more wrong.

My intake counselor, Cynthia, helped me find temporary housing and eventually a permanent place of my own. Not only that, she connected me with a counselor to help me deal with my anxiety and depression and found a class where I could study to get my GED. There were times Cynthia drove me to my GED class when I missed the bus. She called to check on me and sent me little encouraging notes telling me that I could accomplish anything I wanted as long as I put my mind to it. Cynthia told me she would hang in there with me as long as I needed her. As corny as that sounds, it worked.

I just want you to know that last year I completed my degree and training to be a dental hygienist. Now I have a great job, good friends, a support system, and a life that I could never have imagined when I was sitting in jail facing solicitation charges, homelessness, and wondering if my life was worth continuing.

These past years haven't been easy. I'm still in counseling, but for the first time in a long time I have something positive to strive for, and I can see the results of my hard work.

I know Cynthia is no longer with New Hope, but I wanted to let you know that I am grateful for everything! Without you guys, I don't know where my life would be. Thank you from the bottom of my heart!"

Touched by what she read, Ilsa again leaned back in her chair, this time thankful for the reminder of why she did what she did. She could deal with Grant, staff resignations, and general tiredness, she thought. The rewards definitely outweighed the sacrifices. And with that, she gathered her things and went home, grateful for today's win.

CHAPTER NINE

Over the next few weeks, Ilsa managed to see Dominic a few times for coffee before she went to work, occasionally for lunch, whenever the restaurant wasn't too busy, or when he could arrange to have someone cover for him while he was gone. She hadn't yet met his general manager, Lu, but Dominic remarked how appreciative he was of her during the times she managed the restaurant while he was away—and so was Ilsa. Ilsa had also learned to look forward to Mondays when the restaurant was closed.

After a long, tiring week, she wanted to see Dominic, but it was Friday night and the restaurant would be very busy. In addition to the regular business they pulled in on the weekends, tonight there was also a private party. All hands were needed on deck, Dominic's hands included.

Since she couldn't spend time with Dominic, it seemed like a good time to catch up with her sisters. As was her routine when she wanted to chat with them at the same time, Ilsa dialed her oldest sister, Ivy, first, then her youngest sister, Imani. She hadn't spoken to them together in a few weeks and missed their talks.

She tried to talk to her sisters as often as she could, but they had demanding careers and families with extra responsibilities vying for their time and attention. At least they managed to keep in touch by text and email as often as they could.

"Hey, ladies, what's been going on?" Ilsa asked, kicking off the conversation.

"I'm glad you called. Haven't heard from you in a while. Before I forget, the plans for Dad's birthday party are in full swing. The deposit has been put down on the caterers, we reserved the community center, and I emailed the menu. Let me know what you think. Need I remind you that we're going to need you to come home early to help? Whatever is going on in your life, don't let it keep you from Dad's big day," Ivy said, then whispered something that sounded as if it was meant for one of her children.

"Wow. That was a lot at one time." While Ilsa was used to Ivy's habit of saying everything she was thinking all at once, at times it was a little much.

Imani chimed in. "Dad said not to make a fuss about his birthday, but I think he's going to be very surprised by the party we have planned. I'm not trying to make you feel guilty or anything, and I know you've been tied up with extra responsibilities at work, but he'll be so happy to see you, Ilsa." Imani knew their father loved them all, but she also recognized that Ilsa was his favorite, probably because she had been the biggest tomboy as a child and used to spend hours with him in the dirty garage getting all covered with grease and dirt from working on his old car.

"Of course I'll be there," Ilsa said, feeling more than a little guilty. "I've been meaning to come home more, but work has been a little tough lately. The new director is a bit challenging to work with and seems hell-bent on undoing all the good things we've managed to accomplish these past years. I truly believe he thinks his job is to second-guess every decision that's ever been made. I'm afraid if he's left alone in the office for any length of time, there won't be anything of New Hope left to salvage."

"Did you ever find out why the board chose him, of all people? In my opinion, you were the one they should have hired for that position." Ivy again whispered something not meant for her sisters to hear.

"Ivy, please tell my nephews that you are busy talking to your sisters, and they need to give you a few minutes of peace and quiet," Imani demanded. Although the youngest, Imani was the most direct of the three sisters. She didn't hold her tongue and had very little patience for foolishness, as she frequently reminded them all.

Ilsa laughed. She had wanted to tell Ivy the same thing but didn't want to hurt her feelings. That didn't appear to concern Imani.

"The board was looking for some fresh ideas or a new direction or some other lame-sounding reason. Doesn't matter at this point. I'm playing the hand I was dealt."

"Mom has been asking us if we've checked on you since the wedding. She wants to make sure you're not working yourself to death or pining away in the house all by yourself."

"Really, Ivy, pining away? I've told Mom time and time again that I have a very full life with plenty of friends and activities to keep me busy. Actually, it was just last week that I had this conversation with her."

"So is anyone in particular keeping you busy these days?" asked Imani, being again direct and to the point.

"As a matter of fact, Miss Nosey, someone is."

"Who?" Imani and Ivy asked in surprised unison.

Ilsa smiled as she imagined the expressions on her sisters' faces.

"Details, Ilsa, details," Imani ordered.

"His name is Dominic, and I met him at the restaurant he owns here in town."

"When did all of this happen and why are we just hearing about it?"

"We've only been going out for a little while, but—"

"But what?" they both nearly shouted.

"But I already think this guy is pretty special. I don't know how to explain it. All I can say is the time we spend together is nothing short of amazing. We have so much fun together, and he treats me like a queen. Not like putting me on a pedestal or anything—more along the lines of being thoughtful, kind, and treating me as if I matter in his life. On top of that, he's smart and funny and *sooooo* sexy. I think I had actually forgotten how fun dating can be. I like him a lot," she added.

"Who are his people?" Ivy asked, barely able to contain her laughter. When they were younger, this was something their parents always asked their daughters about any boy they liked enough to mention. The girls hated that question, knowing their parents couldn't possibly know everyone. Plus, the question sounded so old-fashioned.

Ilsa knew her sister was joking but wondered if she should mention that Dominic's people looked nothing like them.

"Ilsa, this is the first time I've heard you say those things about anyone other than Quinn."

"I know," she said quietly. "There hasn't been anyone worth mentioning before. It helps that we spend a lot of time talking and getting to know each other. He even sends me text messages letting me know that he's thinking about me. I'm kind of embarrassed to admit it, but when I get those messages I start grinning like I'm twelve years old."

"There's nothing wrong with that," Ivy replied.

"We also do a lot of fun things that I haven't taken the time to do over the past year, like going to the movies, for walks, out dancing, and dinner. The funny thing is that no matter what we're doing, it feels good and right and special. Like I said, there's something special and different about Dominic that makes me excited to see him and miss him when we aren't together."

"Sounds to me like this man knows how to put a smile on your face," Ivy remarked.

"For now," Imani said, with more than a hint of skepticism. "Have the two of you slept together yet?"

"Imani!" This time it was Ivy and Ilsa who spoke in unison.

"Why would you ask her that?"

"Please, Ivy. You know how men can be. They wine and dine you until they get the panties. Then it's *adios*. On to the next lonely woman."

"Look, Imani, that may have been what happened to you before you met Andre, but even you have to admit there are still some good men out there. If anything, your husband should be a true testament to that statement," Ivy scolded.

Imani agreed. "He is. It's just that Ilsa hasn't had more than one or two dates with the same man in years. I don't want her to get burned like I did before I wised up. Let's be realistic; men tend to think that women over a certain age should feel lucky to have their attention, especially since the older men get, the younger they want their partners. The bottom line is I just want Ilsa to be safe and happy."

"Hello, I'm still on the line," Ilsa chimed in. "Please stop talking about me as if I can't hear you."

"Look," Imani continued, "I don't want you to get so caught up that you miss any red flags. Like I said, safe and happy is the goal. I can't stress that enough. If this Dominic makes you happy then it's all good. Just be careful and be smart. Protect your heart. Remember, don't give so much of yourself away that if things don't work out, then you're left with nothing but a broken heart, crushed spirit, and regret."

"And on that happy note, I've got to go, ladies. I just heard something fall, and the boys have gotten very quiet. Love you." And with that, Ivy dropped off the call.

"I'm not trying to be mean or cynical. You know I love you. More than anyone I can think of, you deserve some happiness. Keep me posted on Mr. Wonderful. And when you decide to give up the goods, use protection!"

After catching up with Imani a little while longer about her job, husband, and children, Ilsa was left alone with her thoughts. Imani could be a little jaded at times, but for the most part she was practical. Ilsa thought about what she had said. Her little sister had warned her to protect her heart. Should she? There wasn't anything Dominic said or did that set off any alarms, and she had no reason to think he would ever hurt her. But in the back of her mind, her sister's words played over and over. *Protect your heart.*

CHAPTER TEN

"Are you awake?"

Eyes still closed, Ilsa clutched her phone and cleared her throat. "Barely."

"Want some breakfast?"

Ilsa took her cell phone away from her ear and checked the time. Seven ten. "Why are *you* awake? I thought the restaurant was busy last night. Shouldn't you still be in bed?"

"It was and I'm not. I just felt like getting up early. I wanted breakfast, and I would love for you to join me."

She couldn't argue with that. "Okay, but you've got to give me a few minutes to shower and get dressed."

"I'm in your driveway. You've got fifteen minutes."

Dominic ended the call before she could protest the very strict time limit he'd set. Didn't he know it took more than fifteen minutes to pull her look together?

Dragging herself out of bed, Ilsa shuffled to the bathroom. Taking one look at herself in the mirror brought a frown to her face. Her hair was a mess, and she would need to do some quick and fancy work to make it and the rest of her presentable in fifteen minutes. Dominic better be glad she liked him enough to make the effort.

Walking back into her room freshly showered and wrapped in a towel, Ilsa checked her phone. She had a text message from Dominic. It read *Tick-tock, time's almost up.* At the end of the message was a smiley face wearing a cheesy grin.

She hoped wherever they were going for breakfast didn't require anything fancier than jeans and a t-shirt. Grabbing bottles of oils and lotions from her dresser, she mixed a concoction of orange, lemongrass, and sandalwood. The perfect scent for a casual Saturday morning.

Checking her reflection in the mirror she was pretty satisfied with the final results, except for her hair. Her cell phone signaled a new text message. Checking it, she saw another message from Dominic. *Time's up, buttercup!*

After a few more minutes Ilsa stepped around the side of her house to the driveway and broke into a big smile. Holding a single sunflower, Dominic leaned against the

Camaro. Unshaven, wearing dark sunglasses, a t-shirt, and jeans, he looked too sexy for words.

"Don't you look absolutely edible," he said, lowering his sunglasses.

"Imagine how good I would have looked if I hadn't been rushed."

Stepping into his arms, Ilsa wrapped her arms around his neck and pressed her lips against his. She liked kissing him and never hesitated to initiate or reciprocate. She didn't know where this aggressive, *take what you want* Ilsa came from, but she liked her.

Ending the kiss she stepped back and took the sunflower and gave him a questioning look.

Dominic inhaled the blend of fragrances she was wearing and exhaled. Whatever she had mixed that morning was intoxicating. "It was the least I could do since I woke you up so early. By the way, I love the look."

Besides the jeans and black t-shirt she had donned for their outing, Ilsa had wrapped her hair in a colorful scarf, letting the curls cascade out of the top. A touch of coral lipstick and silver hoop earrings completed the look.

"What are you doing?" she asked when Dominic took her hand and led her to the open door on the driver's side.

"You're driving."

She didn't need to be told again. With a squeal of excitement, Ilsa seated herself in the driver's seat, cranked up the Camaro's engine, and peeled out of the driveway.

Merging onto the highway, Ilsa shifted into high gear, accelerating smoothly but aggressively. It was still early so there wasn't much traffic, which was a good thing. The posted speed limit was sixty-five, which Ilsa took into strong consideration as she raced down the highway. Expertly taking a few bends and turns in the road with the precision of a race car driver, she more than handled the Camaro as if she'd been driving it her entire life.

After she'd had her fill and begin to feel hunger pangs, Ilsa pulled back onto the city streets. "Where to now?" she asked, quite satisfied with the exciting driving experience.

"Let's go by the restaurant, speed demon."

Carefully driving down the narrow street that led to the restaurant, Ilsa pulled into the empty parking lot.

"I was tempted to do a donut," she joked.

"The way you peeled out of your driveway, I was prepared for anything."

Dominic unlocked the door to the back of the restaurant and turned off the alarm. Once inside, he turned to Ilsa who seemed puzzled. Leaning in to give her a quick kiss on the lips, he said, "Now that my nerves have settled after that *exhilarating* ride, I can't think of a better place to have breakfast than here at the restaurant."

Ilsa stepped into the gleaming kitchen and looked around at all of the gadgets and equipment neatly stored on counters and shelves. "Wow. So this is where the magic happens." Until now she had only been in the main dining area and Dominic's office.

Dominic went into the cooler to retrieve everything they needed to make breakfast. Joining Ilsa back at the prep area, he asked her to prepare the fruit—papayas, strawberries, raspberries, and blueberries. While she was busy, Dominic worked beside her beating eggs and chopping vegetables for western-style omelets.

"Wait," he said. "Something is missing."

Ilsa looked around to see what he was talking about. They certainly didn't need any more food. She had serious doubts that they would be able to eat everything they were already preparing.

Dominic went into the small pantry. The next thing she knew, the kitchen was filled with music.

"Now. That's better," he said, rejoining her. Planting another kiss on her cheek, he lingered briefly to once again inhale her heady scent, sparking images of sun-soaked, carefree summer days to come to mind.

They continued to work side-by-side, laughing, talking, and sampling bits of fruit and vegetables. Ilsa finished rinsing and cutting up the fruit and placed everything in the bowls Dominic had provided. She watched as he chopped meat and vegetables with the precision of a master chef.

"I could never do that without chopping off at least one finger," she observed, in awe of his technique.

Dominic laughed. "Yes, it does take practice. I've got the scars to prove it. But I'm sure you could master this easily with a little instruction."

Handing her the knife, he motioned for her to come closer. Standing behind her, Dominic placed his hand over hers and in slow motion guided her in the proper chopping technique.

Ilsa struggled to concentrate on what Dominic was saying but was so distracted by how close they were, she almost completely missed the onion with the blade of the knife.

"Try again," he urged.

Ilsa tried again but with the same results. Unable to focus, she decided to try a third time which ended just as badly as the first two attempts. Distracted by Dominic, she could practically feel his body heat engulf her, sending her emotions into overdrive. The way he wrapped his body around hers while offering instructions did nothing more than turn her into a klutzy mess.

Her throat felt dry, but the rest of her body reacted to this beautiful, sexy, and completely masculine specimen who, at the moment, happened to be occupying every inch of her personal space. Dropping the knife, she maneuvered herself around to face Dominic.

"I have to confess, normally I'm not this much of a klutz in the kitchen. It's just that you, I mean I can't..."

Equally affected, Dominic knew exactly what Ilsa was struggling to say. He, too, lacked the words to express what he felt, but he knew the right action to take. Leaning in to nuzzle her neck, he placed the lightest kiss just below her right ear.

"You..." she said, unable to finish her thought when he reached under her t-shirt and placed his hands on the small of her back, pulling her closer to him.

"Yes?' he whispered, barely touching his lips to hers.

Giving in to the sexy play Dominic had ignited, Ilsa leaned in, placing her hands on both sides of his face, and deepened the kiss. Not only did she love kissing him, she loved the way he reciprocated. She didn't even mind the scratchiness from his unshaven face. In fact, she kind of liked it.

Their bodies, pressed together, fueled the desire that had been building between them. Dominic's hands teased and caressed her back, sending showers of sparks throughout her entire body. His hands were rough, but she didn't mind. In contrast, they were also gentle and felt good against her skin, igniting something deep within her.

In one swift motion, Dominic turned her around and away from the prep table. Ilsa didn't quite know how she ended up there, but she found herself sitting atop a small desk situated between the cooler and a large shelf. Taking advantage of her position, she wrapped her legs around Dominic's waist and pulled him as close to her as possible.

He could feel her hardened nipples pressed against his chest. "Are you trying to drive me crazy?' he asked breathlessly.

"Yes," she said seductively. "I also want to show you a few other interesting things to do in the kitchen."

With the music playing and Dominic and Ilsa entangled in each other's arms, oblivious to everything else, they didn't see or hear Milo, the restaurant's sous chef, standing just inside the kitchen. Clearing his throat again, he remained unnoticed. Not knowing any other way to get his boss' attention he "accidentally" knocked a small metal pan to the floor.

Startled, Dominic swung around to see what was going on. "Milo, what the hell are you doing here?" he asked angrily while at the same time shielding Ilsa.

Mortified, Ilsa peered over Dominic's shoulder. A very embarrassed man, wearing a t-shirt with the restaurant's logo, looked as if he wanted to be swallowed up into the floor. She could relate.

"I wanted to come in early and get everything ready for the new guy starting today," he said apologetically.

Dominic had completely forgotten about the new cook starting. He felt Ilsa tap him on the shoulder in what he hoped was her signaling that she had put herself back together.

"Sorry, Milo. That completely slipped my mind," he said in a tone that lacked the anger from a few seconds earlier.

Milo nodded, not trusting himself to speak. At this point, he felt anything he said would make the situation even more awkward than it already was.

Dominic grabbed Ilsa's hand and pulled her from behind. "Milo, I'd like you to meet someone. This is Ilsa Tanner."

Milo stepped forward and extended his hand. "Nice to meet you."

"And you," Ilsa replied, feeling sorry for Milo who couldn't even look her in the eye.

Dominic turned to Milo. "If you could excuse us for a few minutes, we're going to finish up here...cooking," he quickly added. "We're going to finish cooking. Then the kitchen will be all yours."

Grateful for the escape, Milo dashed out of the kitchen to another part of the restaurant.

Dominic looked apologetically at Ilsa and stroked her face with the back of his hand. "I am so sorry."

"Don't be. I think Milo was way more embarrassed about this than we were," she said. "At least your staff will have something interesting to talk about later."

The look on Dominic's face let her know he was less than pleased with that idea.

Dominic quickly finished preparing the meal, plated it, and led Ilsa to his office. He had no idea where Milo had disappeared, but he was fine not seeing him.

Sitting in his office, he and Ilsa finished their breakfast. Although still embarrassed, they were both able to laugh about what had happened earlier.

"I'm not sure if I feel worse for myself or poor Milo. The man looked as if he wanted to die."

Dominic nodded. He could only imagine what Milo would have walked in on just a few minutes later.

On the drive home, Ilsa turned to Dominic and smiled. "Thank you for everything today. I had fun. I even enjoyed our little breakfast adventure."

"You're not upset with me for putting you in that awkward situation, are you?"

"Nope. You forget I was very much a willing participant."

Dominic reached over, grabbed her hand, and pulled it to his lips. "Then we will absolutely have to do it again."

"By the way, I have a name for your car."

"Already?"

She nodded. "I hereby dub this beauty *Bella*."

Dominic smiled. A perfect name. And a perfect day.

CHAPTER ELEVEN

Ilsa checked her afternoon schedule. She was supposed to meet Tia Phillips to discuss the details of the computer training program. Normally one of the intake counselors would have met with Tia, but lately they were so understaffed, everyone pitched in where they could. Unfortunately, she wasn't confident Tia would show up. Tia had canceled and rescheduled at least three appointments.

While she waited to see if she would show up, Ilsa used the time to catch up on email. As she continued clearing out her email box, Grant stepped into her office.

"Do you have a minute?" he asked, then took a seat before she could answer.

"Well, I have an appointment with a client. Since she hasn't arrived yet, I guess I do have a few minutes. What can I help you with?" she asked, doing her best not to let Grant see how much his very presence annoyed her.

"Have any of the clients qualified for or shown any interest in the computer training program?"

It bothered Ilsa that he never referred to the women as "our" clients. She also couldn't remember one time he had ever interacted with any of the women, not even to say hello. Maybe he didn't fully grasp that their clients weren't merely a group of people with whom they had no connection. These were women with whom most of the staff had developed personal relationships in addition to investing time, the center's resources, and their personal energy into helping them build better lives.

"It's funny you should mention that. I have someone coming in this afternoon who I think would be a good candidate."

"Really? Is she the only candidate?"

Ilsa nodded. "I think we can get more of the women involved, but the time commitment for the program has been a problem. Participants need to attend classes for thirteen weeks."

Grant looked oblivious. "Thirteen weeks? Is that all? That shouldn't be too hard to commit to."

Clueless.

"It is when you don't have a support system, a way to get to and from training, or if you're already working two jobs and still aren't able to make ends meet."

"Well, I don't think we should spend too much time pushing this program, especially if the women don't see the value in it and aren't taking advantage of what is being offered."

"It's kind of up to us to help them see the value in what we are offering. For a lot of these women, a career in the IT field is an opportunity to pull themselves out of poverty with a good-paying and stable job. The bonus is that some of the positions available to them, once they finish the program, would allow them to work from home."

She continued because she had grown tired of Grant thinking that all New Hope needed to do was to find housing for the women instead of taking the next steps and helping them to break out of the cycle of poverty that they often found themselves in.

"If we don't do more than provide housing for our clients, then we haven't done all we can for them. Helping them to see and reach their potential by introducing them to careers that will provide safe and stable housing, a steady income, and a sense of purpose is just as important. I get that not everyone can commit to thirteen weeks of training in addition to working their other job or jobs, but we have women who have become electricians, welders, call-center representatives, nurses, vet techs, entrepreneurs, and countless other professions that they never dreamed of seeing themselves in, all because these great folks here at New Hope see their potential and do whatever they can to help our clients reach that potential."

Grant stood, shrugging. "If you say so. I don't want the staff here spending time and funding on anything that doesn't give a good return on the dollars we invest in the clients."

Ilsa took a deep breath and watched as Grant left her office. A thousand retorts swarmed around in her head and threatened to spill out with a fury she had not experienced in a long time, but she successfully held her tongue.

Leaning back in her chair looking up at the ceiling, she wondered how someone like Grant navigated through the world without the slightest bit of empathy or even the hint of a clue. Once, she had to explain to him why one of their clients, a nineteen-year-old who had been in foster care for nearly all her life, struggled with the reality of living as an adult when no one had ever taught her how to be an adult. Basic skills such as opening a bank account, understanding and signing a lease for a new apartment, navigating college admissions, and setting up utilities were overwhelming and confusing for this young woman.

Fortunately, New Hope had a program for young women transitioning out of foster care. In this instance, they were able to provide services to place her on a path to becoming a productive and stable adult. Ilsa knew that a few staff members still kept in contact with her and, by all accounts, she was doing well.

This was in stark contrast to Grant's initial suggestion to find her a place to stay and encourage her to apply at one of the many fast-food restaurants that were always hiring, his idea of a steady job for "someone like her." He expressed that she would figure the rest out for herself.

Unbelievable.

Once again, instead of wasting any more of her time trying to figure Grant out, she decided to focus on doing the best she could for the women who came through the doors of New Hope. That alone would have to be enough for now.

CHAPTER TWELVE

"Talk me off the ledge, please!"

Dominic mouthed something to Lu and went into his office, closing the door behind him. "What's wrong?"

Ilsa did her best to tamp down the frustration that welled up and threatened to turn into full-blown anger, but she wasn't very successful. "This man is driving me and the staff completely nuts!"

"What's he done now?" Dominic had heard stories of New Hope's director and his general ineptness. He, too, wondered how and why he had been selected for the job, although he pretty much knew the answer. After working in the corporate arena for many years, he knew it wasn't always an individual's skills that landed them the top jobs; it likely might be who they knew in positions of power.

"Almost from day one he has questioned practically every decision that was in place before he ever got here. I understand wanting to make improvements and increase efficiency, but he has done none of that. The sad truth is he understands very little about the actual work we do at the center, and he speaks in abstracts about everything. His solution to everything is to find the women housing, give them a food card, bus voucher, and move on to the next client with no regard for what the women need the most. According to him, everything we do and every service we offer should be measured in dollars and cents. He actually asked me to come up with a report that will measure the return on investment from our clients. *He wants me to show this in dollars and cents!* We already have metrics showing how our programs perform and how we spend our funds. That isn't good enough, I guess. Now he wants us to take each client and calculate how much we invested in them—every phone call, meeting, email—and determine if the investment paid off."

"How do you measure the success of someone who had to go to rehab ten times before they stayed clean? What dollar amount would be reflected in a single mother, who had previously been living in her car with her children, now having a stable place to live and job where she earns enough to support her family?"

Ilsa shook her head, once again trying to make sense of Grant's request. "Now the pep talks, calls to check up on a client, and even the occasional encouraging email or text should be accounted for. Oh, I forgot to mention, he wants three years' worth of data. Three years is a lifetime for some of these women. Some have moved on to bigger and better things; some have disappeared. It's not unusual for some clients to move and end up scattered all over the country with no forwarding addresses. There's no way to follow up with them. Trust me, we've tried. We know where the majority of our current clients are living and how they're doing. Overall, I feel we do a pretty good job of keeping track of the women we serve to make sure they are receiving the necessary services to get off and stay off the street and into decent, good-paying jobs. With that said, how do you put a dollar value on those services?"

"What can I do to make this better?" Dominic felt for Ilsa. Having to deal with someone so clueless day in and day out had to be draining. He knew there wasn't much he could do except to listen, something he sensed she needed at the moment.

An audible and very tired-sounding groan came through the phone.

"Nothing," she said wearily. "I just needed to vent. I'm sorry to be such a downer. I hope at least you're having a good day."

"You're not a downer, and my day has been uneventful. So, are you off the ledge yet?" he asked, hoping to interject a little humor.

"Temporarily."

"Well, I might have the perfect distraction."

"What? I could certainly use one of those right about now."

"You've been so focused on work that you've forgotten Labor Day is in a few weeks."

Dominic heard rustling papers and voices in the background on Ilsa's end. She must have covered her phone with her hand because he could hear her talking, but her voice was muffled.

"I'm sorry. What's in a few weeks?"

"Labor Day."

"You're right, I had forgotten. Is the restaurant still going to be closed that Monday?'

"Yes, which brings me—"

Before he could finish the sentence, Ilsa cut in. "Sorry, I've got to run. Priscilla is standing in my doorway waving a piece of paper. She's smiling, so I'm hoping it's something good. I'll call you later. Thanks for keeping me sane."

Dominic leaned back in his chair and sighed. He had missed the opportunity to ask Ilsa something very important. Now he would have to find another time, but it would have to be soon.

—*ele*—

With her open laptop resting on her lap, Ilsa stared at the screen into a blank spreadsheet. She tried to come up with a way to pull the report together that Grant had asked for, but no matter what she managed to come up with, there were missing pieces that made the information she needed to summarize incomplete.

The time in the bottom corner of the laptop screen read nine-fifteen. She had spent all day working on this report and still had nothing useful to satisfy Grant. The recycle bin on her desktop was filled with failed attempts. She had hoped that after coming home, getting something to eat, and relaxing for a bit, she'd be able to look at things with a different perspective, but nothing had changed and she had to have something to show Grant the next day.

Checking the time again when she heard the doorbell ring, she wondered who could be at her door at this hour.

Before releasing the lock and opening the door, she asked, "Who is it?"

"It's the big bad wolf," came the reply from the other side.

Ilsa opened the door to see a smiling Dominic standing on her porch. With just the hint of beard stubble and a fresh haircut, he looked incredibly delicious. Spending time with him would be way better than plugging numbers into a spreadsheet, except realistically she needed to put work first.

"Since when does the big bad wolf come bearing gifts?"

She stepped aside to let him in but not before taking from his hand one of the bags he was holding.

Dominic put his free arm around Ilsa's waist and pulled her close to his body. He leaned down and gently pressed his lips to hers. She looked as if she needed a hug.

His kisses were always welcome, and this time was no exception. Warm, sweet, and intoxicating, that small gesture managed to make her feel wanted and appreciated. It wasn't only his kisses either. Every touch, each embrace, and every sweet word had that effect on her.

Once again Imani's question played over in her mind. *Have the two of you slept together yet?*

Her relationship with Dominic was different than any she'd had before. Surprisingly to her, none of it had to do with race. It was their conversations, the time they spent together, and, more importantly, how they spent their time that defined who they were as a couple. Although it had been only a matter of weeks, she had grown very close to him during that time. There wasn't a day that they didn't talk on the phone, text, or see each other. She liked Dominic. A lot. But they hadn't slept together. It wasn't that she didn't want to, and there certainly wasn't any pressure from Dominic. It just hadn't happened yet.

"When you texted me and said you were going to pull an all-nighter getting the report ready for Grant, I thought you might like some provisions. Coffee, sandwiches, and-" he held up a container, "chocolate pudding cake."

Dominic followed Ilsa into the living room where she flopped down on the sofa.

"Since I can't get any work done, I might as well mask my frustration with food." Pushing her laptop aside, she rifled around in one of the bags sitting on the coffee table and found a spoon. Finding what she wanted, she settled back and said, "I'm sure the other stuff you bought is going to be delicious, but let's have dessert first."

He laughed. She was the only person he knew who would occasionally eat dessert before her entrée.

The first time she did that she looked at him unapologetically right before she placed a scoop of banana cream pie in her mouth and remarked, "Life is short. Sometimes you need to eat dessert first."

As Ilsa munched on the chocolate concoction, Dominic glanced at her laptop. "How's it going?" he asked tentatively.

"It's not," she said, taking another spoonful of her dessert.

"Is there anything I can do to help? Or should I go? I don't want to be a distraction."

Ilsa shook her head. "Don't go. I could use the company, plus I have writer's block or spreadsheet block, or whatever you call it when you can't figure out how to do something in a spreadsheet."

Placing her spoon inside the empty container, she slumped back on the sofa. "Ugh! I miss Brenda. She would be able to do this without blinking twice."

"Who?"

"Brenda. She recently resigned from New Hope. She was a whiz at this kind of thing. Clearly, I'm not. I cannot believe how much time and energy I'm spending on this. And what is Grant going to do with it once he has the information? My guess is nothing. He seems to take pleasure in having me create charts, graphs, and complicated reports only to leave them sitting in his inbox or on his desk."

Dominic knew she was probably right, but he encouraged her anyway. "Look, you're a smart lady. I'm sure you can figure this out."

Ilsa picked up a pillow from the sofa, pressed it to her face, and groaned loudly.

"Feel better?"

"Nope. My mind is still blank, and I'm no happier about having to do this than I was five minutes ago."

"Okay, maybe I can help. I was thinking about this on my way over here. How about this: instead of assigning a dollar value to each of the services the center offers, why not assign point values."

"Like what?"

"What client would be considered the most at-risk and would require immediate services?"

"Someone coming out of a shelter without the prospect of permanent housing. Or someone in need of mental health services because they are a danger to themselves or someone else."

"Then those two scenarios would receive a high point value."

Sitting up, Ilsa reached for her laptop and scrolled through some files until she found a spreadsheet listing dates of service, client needs, and client zip codes.

She had already deleted names and other identifying information which didn't necessarily need to be in the report.

"I get it. I can create a pivot table from the scrubbed client data to see how many like or identical scenarios there are. This might be a little more meaningful than reporting on individual clients. From there I can determine what scenarios would be assigned high, medium, or low point values. There may be some caveats that would increase or decrease the points based on whether or not a client has children, a job, transportation, or..." Ilsa's voice trailed off as she stretched out on the sofa, propped up a pillow behind her back, repositioned her laptop, and buried herself in the emerging report.

Dominic cleaned up the dessert containers and took the sandwiches and coffee to the kitchen. Glad he was able to help get the creative juices flowing, he now wondered if he should leave or stay. There wasn't much more he could do at this point. The moment Ilsa brought up pivot tables and macros, he knew he was out of his league.

"Dominic, can you bring me a bottle of water, please?"

Joining her back on the sofa, she looked up with a smile and took the bottle he offered.

"Thanks. Oh, and don't think about leaving. I need you. You're my muse."

And with that, Dominic took a seat on the opposite end of the sofa, placing Ilsa's legs across his lap, and prepared for what could be a very long evening.

CHAPTER THIRTEEN

The first rays of light from the early morning sun filtered into the room. Dominic awoke to find Ilsa fast asleep, legs still stretched across his lap, and her laptop resting on the coffee table. Unsure of who fell asleep first, he knew she had indeed pulled an all-nighter.

Gently holding her legs, he slid off the sofa hoping not to wake her. Standing and stretching to get circulation back in his legs, he checked his watch. Five forty-five. Ilsa was scheduled to meet with Grant at eleven. He debated letting her sleep or waking her and fixing breakfast.

"What time is it?" Ilsa leaned up on her elbows.

Dominic marveled at how beautiful she looked with no makeup, her hair tossed about, and clothes wrinkled from being slept in all night.

"Hey, sleepyhead. I didn't mean to wake you."

"You didn't. I was just taking a catnap. Where were you going?"

He reached down and picked up the blanket that had covered them most of the night but had fallen to the floor at some point. Funny—falling asleep on the couch with just a little throw covering them and in what would normally be an awkward and uncomfortable sleeping position, he woke up feeling just fine. Actually, better than fine.

Then it struck him. Dominic smiled. This was the first time that he and Ilsa had spent the night together. He wondered if she had the same revelation. Not quite how he had imagined it, but the particulars didn't matter very much. He wouldn't change a thing.

"Well," he said, as he knelt, admiring his no-longer-sleeping beauty, "I was trying to decide if I should fix you something to eat or let you sleep." Noticing a cluster of wayward curls falling in her face, he reached out and brushed them back with his hand. He moved closer and pulled her up to meet him in what started as a gentle good morning kiss but quickly intensified when Ilsa wrapped her arms around his neck, deepening the kiss. He welcomed the move, readily giving in as his body reacted to her touch, her scent, and the attraction that simmered between them.

Coming up for air, he wanted nothing more than to continue down the path that would lead them upstairs to her bedroom with him undressing her, touching and kissing her from head to toe, feeling her body next to his, and making love to her with everything he had to give. But he didn't act on what his body begged for. He couldn't. As much as he hated being the voice of reason, he knew he had to be at the moment.

"What's wrong?" she asked, clearly feeling the effects of the kiss, but also noticing his hesitation.

"Did you finish the report?"

Surprised, she asked, "The report? Not yet, but I've got time."

"You need to finish."

He had to be joking, she thought. Ilsa took a deep breath and closed her eyes. Maybe he was teasing her.

Giving him a moment to recant, she looked deep into his eyes, smiling seductively.

Dominic felt his willpower slipping away like a landslide.

Leaning in just inches from his ear, she whispered, "But that's not what I want and neither do you." Punctuating the thought she took his earlobe between her lips, giving it a gentle tug.

Dominic groaned and tried to summon as much of his remaining willpower as possible. It was a difficult task.

No matter what he did to gain control, his body betrayed him by doing the opposite. With each seductive look, well-placed touch, and delicious kiss, he felt almost powerless to resist her advances. Ilsa was not playing fair! At this point, resistance truly was futile.

Taking a moment, he pulled himself together. "Ilsa, I want the first time I make love to you to be more than just a hurried event that happens before we have to head off to work." He traced a finger down the side of her neck to her chest directly over a hardened nipple, circled her breast, and sent sparks shooting through her body. "I want to take my time exploring every inch of you from the top of your head to the tips of your toes. I want to kiss and caress you until your body is begging for me. And then, when you're ready, I'll make love to you in a way that will leave no doubt how much you mean to me and how badly I've wanted you."

Ilsa wasn't sure if he was trying to turn her on or kill the mood. If the latter, his method sucked! His words said one thing, but his touch said quite another.

"Now, I'm going into the kitchen to make us some coffee and breakfast. While I'm gone, you need to finish your work," he gently ordered, pointing to her laptop.

Staring at Dominic as he walked off to the kitchen, Ilsa waited for him to turn back and say, "Just kidding," then take her up to her bedroom and make passionate love to her. He didn't. Once she heard pots and pans banging in the kitchen, she knew he was indeed very serious.

Her first thought was to march into the kitchen, strip naked, and rip off Dominic's clothes. Predictably, he would be so hot and bothered that there would be no other option but to act on their feelings for each other. She knew he would remind her she was supposed to be working. But she wouldn't give him a chance to change her mind. She would straddle him on the kitchen table, sending the salt and pepper shakers crashing to the floor. Then mounting him, she'd feel him deep inside as she rode him for what she knew would be the sexiest and most pleasurable ride of her life, culminating into an orgasmic explosion the likes of which he'd never known.

Ilsa let out a soft moan. As amazing as her fantasy sounded in her head, reality kept her planted on the sofa. Regrettably, she knew what she had to do. Picking up her laptop, she switched it on and continued working on the report, all the while sulking and cutting her eyes in the direction of the kitchen.

Dominic turned on the kitchen faucet full blast, hoping the sound would drown out how heavily he was breathing. Taking a handful of cold water and splashing it on his face, he couldn't believe what he'd done. He leaned over the sink as water dripped from his face, still hot from just moments earlier, he took slow, measured breaths, forcing himself to think of any and everything except the sexiest woman he'd ever known, just feet away, ready, willing, and very much available. And he had walked away from all of that!

It was for the greater good, he reassured himself, not sure if he was truly convinced.

Once the aroma of freshly brewed coffee wafted into the living room, it wasn't long before Dominic came back carrying two mugs.

"I'm almost finished," she announced, no longer annoyed but pleased that she had accomplished what seemed like an impossible task the day before. Even though she wouldn't admit it, she was also secretly pleased that Dominic had pushed her to finish. Sitting up, she positioned the laptop so he could see her work.

Handing her a steaming mug of coffee, Dominic sat beside her on the sofa and leaned over to see what she had created.

"I was able to do a lot of this last night. Let me show you what I have so far." Clicking open the first spreadsheet, she explained, "This is the summary of the scenarios or common client characteristics I came up with based on similarities in the data." She clicked on another tab in the spreadsheet. "I took that information and created these charts. I don't know if Grant wanted charts or not, but he's getting them. He can click on the data elements in the charts and drill down to the details. I'll keep the pivot table to show how many of the different types of scenarios we've had over the past three years. For the women we can't account for because they moved or are off the grid, I created a special category."

Duly impressed, Dominic followed along as Ilsa clicked on one spreadsheet after another. She seemed to be very adept at analyzing numbers and turning those numbers into manageable and useful pieces of information. He didn't understand why she ever doubted her ability to pull this report together, except to blame Grant, whose management style, or lack thereof, was slowly eating away at her confidence.

"The final piece," she announced. She clicked a few cells to demonstrate what she deemed a user-friendly way to access and return the center's data. "There are different reports based on what info the user is looking for. They only need to complete the questions and select data elements from the dropdown list. The result is a custom report based on the common characteristics and demographics of the clients we serve, fiscal year, and point value."

"Bravo!" Dominic clapped and bowed slightly. "How in the world did you ever learn to do all of that?"

Ilsa shrugged. "When you work for a non-profit, you find yourself learning and doing a lot of things that aren't in your job description. As a result, you pick up lots of odds-and-ends skills. Plus, before Brenda left, she showed me a few tricks and tips."

"Impressive. I might have to hire you at the restaurant."

"I don't know if you can afford me," she joked.

"Maybe not, but I do have something for you after all that hard work. A reward."

Ilsa saved and closed her work. "You do?"

Standing to his feet, Dominic pulled her up to meet him. He kissed her, running his tongue along her coffee-flavored lips. "I do," he responded, his voice husky and seductive. "It's breakfast, and I've laid it out in the kitchen, all hot, delicious, and waiting to be devoured."

Ilsa punched him playfully in the arm and followed him into the kitchen for her "reward."

Dominic stood with Ilsa in the driveway, sending her off with a passionate kiss to face Grant, a travel mug filled with her favorite blend of coffee, and a promise to meet after work.

As he watched her drive away, he made a promise to himself. Tonight. He would ask her tonight. He truly hoped she would say yes.

CHAPTER FOURTEEN

"Hello, Mom."

"Hello, son. To what do I owe this surprise call?"

Bull's eye! His mother's guilt arrow hit its target. It had been a little while since they'd spoken, and he already felt like a bad son. Her words only cranked that guilt up a notch.

Lately, most, if not all, of his free time had been spent with Ilsa. It was his fault that she didn't know that, leaving his mother to infer that he was busy doing other things and too busy to check on her. Maybe it was time she knew how he was really spending his time.

"You're right. I have been neglectful. And for that, I do apologize."

"*Hmph.*"

More guilt.

"I was calling to see if you'd given any more thought to coming for a visit."

Marta had given it some thought. She missed her son and would love nothing more than to spend time with him. Even though she was busy volunteering and serving on different boards, she enjoyed her time with her children and grandchildren.

"Yes, I have been thinking about it, and I think I would like to spend a few days with your sister first and then come to Columbus. How does that sound?"

"I think that sounds great, Mom. I'll go ahead and make your reservations."

After settling on the dates, Dominic scribbled down his mother's special instructions—no early flights, no red eyes, and she preferred a window seat.

Once he had everything verified they continued to talk for a little while longer before Dominic decided to broach another subject.

"There was another reason I wanted to speak to you today."

"Is everything okay?"

Better than okay. "Yes, everything's fine. I just wanted to let you know that I've met someone."

Surprised by her son's announcement, Marta instinctively knew this "someone" had to be special. Dominic rarely talked with her about any of his friends, particularly the women he dated. When she did manage to pry information out of him about his dating life, he never mentioned names, only the occasional tidbit about taking someone to dinner, a play, or a concert. There hadn't been a special woman in his life since his marriage ended, which made her even more eager to hear about this new woman.

"Tell me about her, Dom. Is she Italian?" she asked, trying not to sound overly excited.

"No."

"Greek?"

"No, but I don't think any of that will matter once you meet her. You'll see that she's kind, compassionate, smart, funny, and very beautiful."

There was no mistaking the affection she heard in his words, spoken and unspoken. As Marta continued to listen, she picked up on something else in her son's voice, something she hadn't heard in a very long time. And she took notice. He was smitten.

"Dom, sweetheart, I cannot wait to meet her. Anyone who makes you this happy is someone I'm sure to love."

"Thanks, Mom."

After they said their goodbyes, Dominic felt an odd sense of relief. Not quite sure how he was going to tell his mother about Ilsa, the words seemed to tumble out all at once as soon as he started talking about her. Surprisingly, the words had come easily—maybe because they reflected everything he felt for Ilsa in his heart.

Dominic hadn't heard from Ilsa all day. He had sent her a text message earlier, but she had yet to respond.

The crowds from earlier in the evening began to dissipate. It was turning into a slow night at the restaurant. Now seemed like a good time to duck out and head to Ilsa's. He checked with Lu before leaving, making sure she was okay with closing.

"Okay, Dominic, we need to talk."

"About?" he asked, looking for something on his desk.

"About what's going on with you."

Dominic stopped his search and looked up to see Lu standing in front of his desk, arms crossed, prepared for a full inquisition.

"I have no idea what you're talking about."

Sighing loudly, she took a seat on the edge of Dominic's desk. "Sooner or later you're going to have to tell me."

"Tell you what?"

"You've met someone, haven't you?"

"What makes you say that?"

"Dom, I swear, if you don't come clean and stop playing with me..."

Sensing Lu was about to hurl something at him, he decided it was time to fess up. "Okay. I was just messing with you." He sat down and focused on Lu. "You're right. I have met someone. How did you know?"

Lu rolled her eyes. "Are you kidding? Every day you're in an unusually good mood. You're all smiley and extra nice to everybody, which isn't a bad thing, but at first, it made me wonder what was going on. Then you started having this lovesick puppy look. Everyone has noticed, believe me. I wasn't going to tell you this, but we heard you humming the other day. Humming! Who hums? And that's not even the strangest thing. Since we've opened the restaurant, I can count on one hand the number of times you've asked me to cover for you. But lately, and I'm not complaining, it's become a common occurrence, especially on Thursdays. What the heck could you possibly be doing on a Thursday? Wait." Lu shook her head and made a face. "Never mind. Forget I asked that. I may not want to know."

Dominic threw his head back and laughed. He wasn't sure where Lu's imagination had taken her, but he was pretty sure he wasn't doing anything remotely close to what she was thinking. The truth was that Thursdays had become his and Ilsa's unofficial date night. He probably wasn't going to share that information with Lu just yet.

"First, let me apologize for cutting out early on Thursdays. I've tried to only do that once the crowds have thinned out. Second, when people are in a good mood, they might occasionally hum. I have nothing more to say about that. And last, but certainly not least, I have no idea what a lovesick puppy looks like, but I can assure you I do not, nor will I ever, resemble one."

Lu made a face. "That's a matter of opinion. Now, let's get back to the real news. Who is this mystery woman, and why haven't you brought her by the restaurant?"

"She's actually been here a few times," he said, thinking back to when Milo caught the two of them making out on the desk in the kitchen. Apparently, Milo hadn't shared the story with Lu or the rest of the staff. "Her name is Ilsa Tanner, and you'll be meeting her soon enough."

"Are those all the details I get? A name? Nothing else?"

Knowing Lu and where she would take the conversation if he let her, Dominic grabbed his cell phone from the desk and asked on his way to the door, "What other details do you need?"

"I don't know. What does she do for a living? What does she look like? Did she like the restaurant? Favorite food? Does she have any pets? Tattoos?"

"That's a lot of information and very random, to say the least."

Realizing she wouldn't get any more details out of her boss, she figured she would try again another time.

"Well, she must be one hell of a woman to take you off the market."

Dominic turned before walking out the door. "She most certainly is."

CHAPTER FIFTEEN

Dominic had barely rung the doorbell when Ilsa snatched open the door. The look on her face instantly told him something was wrong.

Dispensing with words, he reached for her, pulling her into his arms.

Her body was stiff, but as soon as he wrapped her in his arms, she began to relax.

"What happened?"

Ilsa allowed the comfort she felt in Dominic's arms to temper her anger enough to tell him how horrible her day had been.

"Ugh!" she said, stepping away and walking toward the kitchen.

Not knowing what else to do, Dominic followed her. Each step conveyed the anger he knew she was feeling. He had never seen her this way before.

Ilsa took a seat at the table while Dominic stood with his back leaning against the counter, aching to hold her again but waiting for a cue. Ilsa was no wilting flower, and he was careful not to make her feel as if he was trying to swoop in and save the day. He needed to be patient.

She had a cup of tea sitting in front of her, but it looked untouched. Hot tea was her beverage of choice when she needed to unwind, he'd learned—usually chamomile.

"As soon as I got to the office this morning, I could tell something was wrong. Priscilla was at her desk in tears. When I asked her what happened, she said Grant had chewed her out over some silly nonsense that was so minor I'm surprised he wasted his time or hers mentioning it. I cannot understand why he felt as if he had to make a mountain out of a molehill."

Ilsa picked up her spoon and stirred her tea. "I went in to talk to him. I wasn't angry or confrontational. I simply needed him to understand how serious this was. The bottom line, I told him that he should apologize to Priscilla. Do you want to know what he had the nerve to say after that? He said that she was being emotional and should learn how to take criticism. He then said if Priscilla couldn't handle the heat, then maybe she should think about finding a job that wasn't so challenging. How unprofessional and cold is that? If anyone needs to get out and find another job, it's him!"

Continuing to stir her tea, she clanked the spoon against the side of the cup with such force, Dominic was surprised it hadn't broken. That was his cue. Walking over to the table, he sat down and took the spoon out of her hand.

"Is Priscilla okay?"

She nodded.

"Are you okay?"

Ilsa leaned back in her chair and looked at the ceiling. "What am I going to do about this man? He is making our lives a living hell. I have two more people looking to leave the center. Two good people, Dom. And one of them has only been there for three months. We can't afford to lose anyone else."

She hadn't mentioned it yet, but Dominic was curious about the report she had stayed up most of the night working to pull together. He decided to ask. "Did you get a chance to show Grant the report?"

Remembering the ordeal with the report, Ilsa sat straight up in her chair and glared. "When I went in to show him what I'd prepared, he stopped me before I could even open my laptop. He said he didn't need it after all and had decided to go in another direction! After all of that, he didn't even want to see what I had prepared. And to add insult to injury, he had the nerve to pull up the data I had already given him. Data he already had before he asked me to pull this ridiculous report together."

Ilsa threw up her hands. "I don't know if this man is trying to break me, drive me crazy, or maybe he has a death wish. Whatever it is, I don't know how much more I can take. To be honest, right about now I'm ready to put my hands around his throat and choke the life out of him."

Reaching across the table, Dominic took Ilsa's hand in his. Her day had been quite horrible. She looked worn out and defeated, something he was noticing more and more. Tired, frustrated, and angry seemed to be the feelings she carried home these days. Yes, he knew there were still times she felt that she and the staff were making a difference; those were the good days. But far too many times she lacked the joy she once had when talking about her work.

He searched for answers but he didn't know how he could help, except to go to her job and punch Grant in the face. While that wouldn't solve a thing, it would make him feel a whole lot better.

Bringing her hands to his lips, he kissed them. "People like Grant are weak. It's evident that he has no people skills, so he feeds off intimidation and fear. More than likely he's doing all this to hide how inadequate he is at the job. I'd be willing to bet that he also feels intimidated by you."

"I doubt that," Ilsa scoffed.

"I'm sure you run rings around him at the center. Keep in mind, the staff loves and respects you, and practically all of the business alliances that have been formed are because of you. Not to mention, you can do things with a spreadsheet that defy the imagination."

He saw a tiny smile. "Don't let him get the best of you. You're better than him by a long shot. Eventually, his lack of leadership and crappy job performance will do him in."

"If I don't get to him first."

Dominic smiled. Even with everything she had to deal with, she still maintained her sense of humor.

"Stay here," he said. "I want to do something special for you."

Dominic left Ilsa sitting at the table staring at her untouched cup of tea. On his way upstairs he stopped. "Stay right there until I call you."

Ilsa's bathroom off the master bedroom contained a large garden-style bathtub that she rarely used. She said it was because she never had time for a leisurely bath. The funny thing was that the first time he saw the tub, the only thing he could think of was the two of them sharing a sensuous bath.

Rummaging around until he found what he was looking for, Dominic started a bath and added a small amount of bubble bath labeled "Relaxation." She also had bottles labeled "Indulgence," "Purification," "Sleep," and "Soothe." Ilsa had more bottles of oils, lotions, fragrant soaps, and packages of shower bombs—he had no idea what those were—than anyone he knew. Everything was neatly lined up and easily accessible. He was impressed with her vast collection but at the same time curious about what all of the different bottles and jars were used for. One thing he loved was that her skin was soft and radiant, and she always smelled so good. From her hair to her silky skin, he loved her unique and various scents, which he attributed to her vast collection.

Standing at the top of the stairs, Dominic called down to check on Ilsa.

"What are you doing up there?" she asked.

"I'll tell you in a minute. Don't come up yet. Quick question. Do you have any candles?"

"What kind?"

"I just want plain old candles. How many kinds are there?"

Ilsa smiled. Sometimes he could be such a man. "If you're looking for scented candles, they're on the top shelf of the linen closet. If you want basic candles, those are under the sink."

After a few more minutes, Dominic came downstairs. Ilsa was still sitting at the table, looking completely defeated.

Taking her hand, he said, "Come with me."

Too tired to protest, she followed as Dominic led her to the master bathroom. The lights were out, but several lighted candles were placed around the room, adding a soft glow.

She turned to him and smiled. "I never use that tub," she said, noticing the filled bathtub.

"I know, but you're going to tonight. Now, I'm going downstairs to make you a fresh cup of tea. When I get back I want to see you up to your neck in bubbles."

Dominic went downstairs and Ilsa complied. The idea of a hot bath really did sound like a good idea. She quickly undressed and stepped into the tub filled with warm, but not quite hot, water and billions of luxurious bubbles. Dominic must have found her collection of bubble bath that she had purchased but never used. She turned on the faucet and added more hot water.

Closing her eyes, she sank, allowing the water to envelop her in its warmth and soothing fragrance.

Slowly, she began to feel some of the day's stress melting away.

"Is that better?'

Ilsa turned to see Dominic walking toward her carrying a steaming cup of tea.

"Yes," she said. "By the way, just in case I become so relaxed that I fall asleep or something, I just want to say thanks."

"For?"

"For giving me space and time to vent about Grant when I need to. For being my muse. For making me use this tub. And for taking care of me, especially when I didn't recognize that I needed to be taken care of."

"You're welcome for all of that." He placed the cup on the side of the tub. "Where's your soap?"

Ilsa took a sip of tea. Chamomile. Perfect. With her head leaning on a towel Dominic had rolled up for a headrest and her eyes closed, she pointed toward the hallway. "Look in the linen closet. There's some lavender and vanilla soap I've been saving for a special occasion."

Dominic rummaged around until he located the special occasion soap and returned to the bathroom. "Where do you get all of this stuff? Your skin and hair care collection puts mine to shame. You'd probably be horrified to know that my shampoo doubles as my body wash."

Keeping her eyes closed and her head resting against the towel, she smiled. "Sounds completely primitive. We'll have to do something about that. I'll talk to my lady."

"It's just one person, not a corporation?" he asked, half-joking.

"Yup, just one lady. She was one of our clients from several years back. She makes and sells all of this. At one time she and her two children were living out of her car. She came to us for help, and we were able to get them into an apartment and help her find a job. After that, during the day, she worked at a warehouse. In the evening she created and sold a line of body oils, lotions, soaps, candles, and hair care products for women with natural hair. Now she has a business of her own."

"Natural hair?"

"Hair that's not been chemically altered," she explained.

Dominic put some soap in the palm of his hand, working it into a nice lather. Placing a towel under his knees for cushion, he leaned over the side of the tub, gently massaging Ilsa's shoulders.

"Mmm...that feels nice. Now I know why cats purr." Dominic's touch felt just right. Her tired muscles relaxed as his gentle fingers massaged out the tension that had rested on her shoulders all day.

"Your fingers are magic," she said, "but I need something, if you don't mind. Something is missing."

"What?" He wondered what he could have forgotten.

Ilsa opened her eyes and smiled. "You. In here. Now."

Dominic raised an eyebrow. "Is that an invitation?"

"No, it's an order."

"Are you sure about this?" he asked, not knowing what would happen but pretty sure they would end up doing more than sharing a bath.

Ilsa sat up and looked at him as the soft glow of candlelight illuminated her face. "Dominic, you have two minutes to get naked."

CHAPTER SIXTEEN

Ilsa paid close attention as Dominic removed each piece of clothing. First, the shirt. Once off, she noticed toned shoulders and arms, a broad chest, and flat stomach. Then the pants, revealing boxer briefs and strong, toned legs. Dominic's hesitation when it came time to remove his boxer briefs brought a smile to her face. He was being modest and appeared to be self-conscious, she thought as she continued to watch.

He blushed.

She loved it!

The glow from the candles provided just enough light for her to see how well Dominic took care of his body. She definitively liked, and was most appreciative of, what she saw.

Dominic tried not to appear nervous. He could see Ilsa checking him out and, for some reason, he was a little self-conscious. He was torn between ripping everything off and quickly getting into the tub or taking his time, hoping Ilsa would stop staring. She hadn't.

"I feel objectified," he said, quickly removing his boxers and walking over to the tub.

"I like your body, and I like that you're ready to play," she teased, never taking her eyes off him. *Oh yes, she liked what she saw.*

Dominic stepped into the water as Ilsa continued to watch his every move. He raised his eyebrows. "I don't remember making the water this hot."

"You'll get used to it."

Adjusting to the temperature of the water and to the realization that he and Ilsa were both naked, mere inches away from each other, Dominic could feel the last bit of his resolve melt away. In his mind, they would enjoy a nice, leisurely bath together, allowing Ilsa to relax and forget the stress of her workday while they talked, laughed, and bathed each other.

Ha! Who was he kidding? Ilsa looked too good to be true, but she was. This, right here and now, was true and real and right. And at this very moment, the only thing he wanted was to touch her, kiss her, and feel her body all over his. He leaned forward. He couldn't think of one good reason to hold back.

"I want to kiss you."

Ilsa smiled. "You don't typically ask."

"I'm being a gentleman."

His tongue, wet and hot, ran over Ilsa's lips, then plunged into her mouth. He could taste the flowery sweetness from the tea on her lips and her tongue. The kiss wasn't meant to be gentle and it wasn't. It was the beginning, the opening of the flood gate of emotions and longing Dominic had been holding back, waiting for the right time, the right place.

So many times he had wanted to make love to Ilsa, but he wanted that first time to be special, not hurried like it had almost been at the restaurant or earlier that morning. He wanted to make her body feel for him what she had felt for no other man. He wanted their first time and each time after to be a reflection of their growing feelings, each time more intense than the time before, holding nothing back and leaving nothing more to give.

He pulled her to him as her slippery body glided effortlessly over his, her breasts pressed into his chest. He broke the kiss and could feel her warm breath against his cheek. Nuzzling Ilsa's neck, Dominic glided his tongue from the base of her throat and back to her lips. Everywhere he licked made him hungry for more. What was it about this woman? He could not get enough of her.

Dominic's hands gripped her waist, slightly digging into her wet, soapy skin. Rising to her knees, Ilsa positioned herself perfectly for Dominic to take one erect nipple in his mouth, then between his teeth.

A slight intake of breath didn't go unnoticed as Dominic's desire clicked up a notch. Her reaction fueled his desire, if that was even possible at this point. His whole body was rigid, hot, and pulsating. The temperature of the water was no match for the heat that welled up in him. He could hear his heart pounding in his ears and feel it thumping in his chest.

Ilsa had tried to contain herself from the moment Dominic stepped into the tub. Truth be told, once he dropped his underwear, she fought to keep from jumping out of the tub and on him. But now, as she straddled him on her knees, there was no holding back. Her body hummed and pulsated with sexual tension. Dominic's kiss had ignited a fuse and there was no stopping the impending flame. She wasn't sure this is what he'd had in mind when he brewed her tea and ran the bath, but she was more than okay with the direction his plans had taken.

Her hardened nipples reacted to every lick, bite, and this amazing thing he did when he wrapped his lips around them. She wanted to feel Dominic inside her so badly while at the same time wanting to savor every moment.

"You are so beautiful," he whispered.

This time she kissed him. Taking charge she relaxed her knees, straddling her legs. Reaching into the water she slowly ran her hands up the insides of Dominic's thighs. She smiled when she heard him moan and was delighted when she found her target hard and ready. In one swift move, Ilsa raised her body slightly and came down on Dominic's waiting erection. Never taking her eyes off him she reached out, holding onto the sides of the tub as she moved her hips allowing every inch of him to fill her.

Grabbing her waist, Dominic moved with her as water splashed and their bodies rocked. He knew they were making a mess, but he didn't care. His only thought was the intense feeling of pleasure escalating, the incredibly erotic way Ilsa gyrated her hips, and the need to hold on to her for dear life. Just when he thought he couldn't hold on any longer, he felt his body tense. Ilsa reached for him. He plunged deeper. She gasped. Then a crescendo of pleasurable sensation and raw emotion erupted from a place that had long been neglected and, for them both, unlike anything they had ever experienced.

Later that evening Ilsa snuggled next to Dominic. For the first time that day, her cares and worries no longer plagued her thoughts. At the moment, her mind was occupied with other thoughts—how good it felt to be in

Dominic's arms, the touch of his hands, and his sweet kisses. Making love had opened a portal, a universe, where only the two of them existed. It wasn't reality, but much better.

"Ilsa?"

"Hmm?"

"I have something to ask you."

"Mm-hmm."

"Labor Day is next weekend. The restaurant is going to be closed on Monday, and Lu is covering for me part of Saturday and Sunday. I think it would be a good time to do something different."

"Something like what we just did?" she half-joked, still reveling in the afterglow of their good lovemaking.

Dominic chuckled and kissed her on the forehead. "Definitely, yes. But I was thinking about going away for the weekend, just the two of us."

"Okay."

"Really? You'll go away with me? For the whole weekend?"

"The way you just made me feel, I'd go with you to the moon and back."

CHAPTER SEVENTEEN

Looking across her desk at Tia Phillips, Ilsa couldn't tell if she was excited or not about the opportunity to participate in the computer training program.

"Is this something you think you might be interested in?" Ilsa asked hopefully.

Tia shifted in her seat and checked her phone. "I never thought about working with computers. That seems like a nerdy job."

Ilsa smiled. "It's a good career. If it's something you think you would consider, I have to let you know that the program will require that you commit to attending classes for thirteen weeks."

"That's a long time. A lot can happen in thirteen weeks."

"True. It's up to you to make good things happen in that time. So what do you say?"

"What if I can't do the work?"

Ilsa looked over the results of the aptitude test Tia had completed online. She had scored in the exceptional range in math, science, and reading comprehension. Truthfully, there was no reason she couldn't do well in the program. In reality, Tia would probably do well no matter what career she chose. The trick was getting her to express an interest in any area of study.

She was happy to see Tia had her high school diploma even if she hadn't attended college or done anything much since graduation. Following a deadbeat boyfriend from her small hometown in Alabama to Columbus, she had been left to fend for herself after he kicked her out. With no money to get back home and no family to whom she could reach out to for assistance, she needed help.

It made Ilsa sad that someone this bright had gotten caught up in the cycle of working dead-end jobs and hooking up with no good men, with little to no hope for a better life. At least she had landed at New Hope. Everyone there, including Ilsa, would do their best to help her set goals and work toward them.

"Look, the only thing that is required of you is to do your best and to ask for help when it's needed. You're a smart young woman who has a bright future ahead of you. This is one step. I realize it's a big one, but you are not alone. We are here to help."

Tia looked as if she wanted to say, "Yeah, if you say so," but she remained silent.

"What do you say? Are you going to do it?"

Tia checked her phone again and nodded. "I'll give it a try. What have I got to lose?"

Ilsa breathed a sigh of relief. Tia didn't realize it, but Ilsa saw something special in her. Now she just had to get Tia to realize for herself that she was capable of many things. This program that she was about to enter would be one of many good things to come.

After she left, Ilsa made the call to enroll Tia in the class. Making some notations in her file, Ilsa thought about the conversation she'd had with her. Normally, she worked with clients to find out their interests, goals, and what they wanted out of life. That process could go in many different directions, but with Tia, Ilsa had trouble getting anything more than the basics out of her. Tia had no idea what she wanted to do with her life. Working at minimum wage jobs that barely paid the rent but sapped all of her energy, it wasn't difficult to understand why she couldn't see beyond her current situation. Sadly, that wasn't even the most distressing part. Ilsa couldn't help but wonder who was responsible for destroying her self-esteem and who had led her to believe she didn't have the right to hope. Was it the boyfriend who used her until someone else came along?

Could the people she'd met growing up who were in a worse state than her or who didn't want to see anyone doing better than themselves be responsible? It didn't matter at this point since there was nothing Ilsa could do to change her past, but she could certainly help her shape a better future.

Playing a game on her phone to kill time, Denita didn't notice Ilsa enter the restaurant until she flopped down at the table looking as if she'd run all the way from her job.

"Whoa. Take a breath. Relax."

Ilsa took a sip of the iced tea Denita had ordered for her and let out a long, slow breath. "I am so sorry that I'm late. I've been trying to wrap some things up at work and Priscilla is out sick. It's been a crazy day, no, crazy week."

Lately, Denita and Ilsa had spent very little time together, with their only communication being via text message, email, and the occasional touch-base phone call on the way home from work.

"How are you, Dee? I miss spending time with you."

"That's because you're a busy girl these days. You get a man and forget all about your best friend."

"That's not true!" *Or was it?*

Denita shot her friend a look that said otherwise.

"Okay, maybe it's a little true. I can't believe I've turned into one of those women. I'll do better. I promise. Will you forgive me if I pay for lunch?"

"Maybe, but you also have to share the details about what's been going on with you and Mr. Fine."

Ilsa broke into a wide grin but held off on giving Denita any details until after the waiter had taken their order.

"Things between us have been great."

"And," Denita prompted, sensing there was more.

"Okay, I don't quite know how to explain it, but Dominic is...amazing."

"Wow. I wasn't expecting that. In what way?"

"I know this is going to make me sound like he's my first crush, but in every way. The man pampers me and treats me like a queen without treating me like I'm helpless. He values my opinion, encourages me when I need it, and he makes me laugh. It sounds like I'm rattling off a bunch of random things, but the more I think about him, the more things come to mind. Let me give you an example. One night, when I needed to stay up late and prepare something for work, Dom came over with food and coffee and kept me company until I finished."

"Kept you company how?"

"Not like you're thinking. I was stuck trying to figure something out, and he was giving me ideas and encouraging me the whole time. He truly was there to keep me company while I worked. No strings attached. Eventually, we ended up falling asleep on the sofa."

"Before or after he tore your clothes off and made you scream his name?"

Ilsa laughed at Denita's vivid imagination. "I told you we fell asleep on the sofa. Period."

"So, no wild sex with Mr. Fine?"

Ilsa took a sip of tea, purposely making Denita wait for her reply. "Well, yes, but not that night."

"I knew it!"

"Shh. People are staring."

"Okay. I just need a few details. Was it toe-curling?"

"Yes, ma'am!"

"Sexy body, sexy face, sexy moves?"

The waiter appeared with their food at the same time Denita was firing off questions, but he only heard the last one. Embarrassed, he put down the plates, mumbled something, and quickly left.

"Yes, yes, and Y-E-S!"

"So, it's safe to say that judging by the cheesy grin you're wearing, Mr. Fine rocked your world."

"My world and any other alternate universe where another Ilsa Tanner might exist."

Both women laughed.

After her lunch with Denita, Ilsa returned to the office to find that Grant had already left for the day. He'd said something earlier about having an appointment that afternoon. She hadn't paid much attention except to register that he would be out of the office. Lately, she paid very little attention to anything he said or did that didn't directly impact her, the staff, or the center's operations.

To say there was a lot of tension between Grant and the staff would be a gross understatement. From the beginning, he had managed to rub everyone the wrong way and nothing since had changed. And because he seemed uninterested in changing his behavior, there was no end in sight.

Ilsa did her best to keep morale up, but it was wearing heavily on her. At least they had the annual staff appreciation day coming up. This was an event she and the previous director had initiated several years ago. The center would be closed for the day, and the staff would be treated to a catered lunch, participate in some fun, team-building activities, and then be given the remainder of the day off. This year Ilsa would have to do some serious finagling to pull the event off since Grant had turned their once-happy workplace into a toxic environment that everyone endured and quickly escaped after putting in their eight hours. No matter what, she would make it work. She felt as if she owed the staff at least that much.

Aside from employee appreciation day, she had her special break from work to look forward to. A long weekend with nothing to do but relax with Dominic was just what she needed. She had even packed her bag already. Dominic wouldn't be able to leave the restaurant until after six, but he was picking her up after that.

She was excited and a little nervous. Even though she and Dominic spent as much time together as their schedules allowed, they didn't typically spend the night together. This would be different for them, particularly her. She had not spent this much time with a man since her husband. Every relationship she'd had since his death had ended not too long after it had started, never getting to the point of long weekends or overnight stays.

She wasn't into casual sex, so even the physical part of a relationship had been pretty much non-existent for her over the years. But Dominic had made her forget those years. With him, everything seemed fresh and new and oh so special. Making comparisons between her husband and Dominic would be unfair, so she didn't do it. What she'd had with her husband would be cherished for the rest of her life; those memories would reside deep in her heart, untouched by anything or anyone.

Thank goodness the heart is a wonderful thing. For within her heart, she had room enough for Dom.

CHAPTER EIGHTEEN

"When's the last time you talked to Mom?"

"Last week. Why?" Byron asked his big brother.

"Did she mention anything about having a boyfriend?"

"Uh, no. Did she say something to you about that?"

"No," Miles replied. Ilsa's oldest son, the more serious of her boys, was a little miffed that his mother hadn't mentioned this to him either. "Aunt Imani let it *slip* when she told me about Grandpa's birthday party. I wonder why Mom didn't tell us."

"I don't know. Maybe she was waiting for the right time."

"Will there ever be a right time for Mom to tell us she has a boyfriend?"

"Good point."

"You think it's somebody we know?"

Byron couldn't imagine anyone they knew who wasn't married, old, or was good enough to be dating their mother. Then he thought about how hard his mother worked and how much she cared for everyone else. He often wondered if she was taking the time to do things for herself or to enjoy the life she had built. Maybe that's what she was doing now.

"I guess if you look at it from Mom's point of view, this may not be a bad thing. Think about it. You're living out there in Seattle. Me and Patrice are here in Atlanta, closer, but still pretty far away. Mom's all by herself. Maybe it's time that she does something for herself like getting out and meeting different people."

"Maybe. I guess I'd feel better meeting this guy face-to-face. Think she'll bring him to Grandpa's party?"

"Don't know. I guess that all depends on how serious they are and whether or not she wants to introduce him to our crazy family."

"That will certainly be interesting. Until then, if he knows what's good for him, he'd better not hurt Mom, or I'll be on the first thing with wheels on my way to Ohio."

"Yes, Dad. Everything is great. How are you and Mom doing?" Ilsa was careful not to let anything slip about her father's upcoming surprise birthday party. She was thankful they were speaking over the phone and not in person, lest her father pick up on something in her facial expressions. He could always tell when she was trying to hide something.

"You know your mother. She has always been and will continue to be a busy woman. If she's not taking some exercise class, then she's delivering meals to seniors or volunteering at the church. I have to remind her to slow down and take a day off now and then."

"Sounds like Mom." Ilsa admired her mother's commitment to stay active and needed during her retirement. Ilsa hoped to have the time and resources to do the same when she retired, something she wouldn't have to think about for a long time.

"Are you still planning on coming home before the weather turns cold?"

Ilsa smiled. Her father always thought it best to travel during warmer weather as if cars weren't capable of functioning any other time. "Yes, I plan to come home in a few weeks."

Ilsa and her father continued talking about their family, events going on at church, and a variety of other topics that kept them on the phone for quite a while. But then, her father surprised her with his next comment.

"Spoke to Imani last week. She mentioned that you're dating. Said you found a nice young man that you've been spending a lot of time with."

Caught off guard, Ilsa didn't quite know what to say. She had wanted to tell her parents, particularly her father, about Dominic, but she was waiting for the right time. Thanks to Imani, that time was now.

"Uh, yes. I am seeing someone."

"Have the two of you been going out for long?"

She wondered how much Imani had told their dad. Not much, she suspected, since she didn't know very much herself.

Since the cat was out of the bag, now seemed as good a time as any to tell him about her relationship with Dominic. She knew she could speak candidly with her father about her feelings for him.

"We've been going out for most of the summer. I think you would like him, Dad. He has a nice restaurant here in town that serves the best food and he's an excellent cook. We spend a lot of time together laughing, talking, and just being together. I guess you could say we've been getting to know each other. The best part is that everything feels comfortable and exciting all at once."

"Does he have kids or family in town?"

"He's divorced, no kids. He doesn't have any family in town but he is close to his mother and sister. And get this; he restored and owns a '69 Chevy Camaro SS." She stopped talking long enough to take a breath. Feeling as if she needed to tell her father every good thing about Dominic at once, she paused to let it all sink in.

"A '69 Chevy? Like Belle?"

"Yes, like Belle. You would be so impressed with the job he did restoring her. And she drives like a dream. He takes good care of that car, Dad. And he takes good care of me," she added.

Ilsa knew it was ridiculous at her age to still want her parents' blessing, but no matter what her age, she never wanted to disappoint or hurt them in any way. Most importantly, she wanted them to share in her joy.

"I see," her father said. "I think that's good, Ilsa. You've been alone for a long time. I want to see you happy. If this man makes you happy, then that's all an old man can ask for."

Ilsa wanted to cry and hug her father all at the same time. "Thank you, Daddy."

"Take care, sweetheart. I'll see you soon."

Ilsa's mother walked in the door shortly after her husband hung up the phone.

"Who was that?" she asked.

"Ilsa."

Noticing the expression on her husband's face, she asked, "Virgil, is she all right?"

"Yes, honey, she's fine. You might say she's better than fine. We had quite a nice chat."

"Then what is it? You look concerned."

Virgil smiled. "I think our daughter is falling in love."

CHAPTER NINETEEN

"Why can't you tell me where we're going?"

"It wouldn't be a surprise if I told you."

"Why does it need to be?"

"Because I like surprising you."

Unable to come up with a plausible counter-argument, Ilsa decided to let Dominic have his way. She wasn't too pressed about the whole matter anyway. All she cared about was that they would be spending the better part of a three-day weekend together. She also wasn't bothered by the fact that Dominic would have to go to the restaurant for a little while on Saturday and Sunday. She was getting used to his odd work hours. There were some things she needed to complete anyway before returning to work on Tuesday, so she had bought her work laptop and a stack of files to work on. Aside from that, it wouldn't be hard to find something to occupy herself while he was away.

The drive to the surprise destination took them outside of the city. Gradually the landscape changed from urban to the sprawling countryside, complete with rolling hills and vast farmlands.

"I spoke to my father before you picked me up."

"Oh yeah? Did you tell him about me?" he asked, half-joking.

"Actually, my sister beat me to it."

"Your youngest one?"

"Yup, how did you guess?"

"That's exactly what little sisters do. They blab. So what does your father know about me?"

"I told him about Bella."

"Is that all?"

"No, I also told him a few other things like how much fun we have together. We talked about the restaurant. And I might have mentioned a thing or two about how good you are to me."

Dominic looked over and smiled. "I can't wait to meet your family."

Ilsa raised her eyebrows. "Be careful what you wish for. My family can be a lot to handle."

After about another hour Dominic pulled off the main highway. Ilsa saw a sign that read *Welcome to Benton*

Lake. A piece of paradise in Ohio. Benton Lake was one of those podunk towns off the beaten path that wasn't known for anything important, or so she thought. Maybe there was more to the town than she had given it credit for. After all, Dominic had thought enough of it to bring her there. There must be something special about it.

Dominic continued to drive for another ten miles or so and then pulled off again onto a small country road. Ilsa looked around, taking in the beautiful scenery. A wide sparkling lake ran along the length of the road, and as far as she could see were trees. She couldn't imagine where they were going, and for a brief, horror-stricken moment she wondered if Dominic had plans to take her camping. Spending time in a tent, sleeping in a sleeping bag, even if Dominic was right beside her, did not translate into the fun, relaxing weekend she had envisioned.

It had begun to get dark, but there was still enough light for Ilsa to take in the natural beauty of the lake and its surroundings. As she continued to survey the area, she saw something just ahead. What looked like a small cabin sat back amongst a bank of trees, nestled in a very private spot within the woods. She let out a small sigh of relief. It wasn't a tent.

Dominic pulled up to the cabin and turned off the car's engine. He glanced at Ilsa, attempting to gauge her reaction.

"We're staying here?"

"Do you like it?" he asked pensively.

She turned to him and smiled. "It's our very own private hideaway in the middle of all this beauty, and it's not a tent," she said gesturing. "Yes, I like it very much."

Relief flooded Dominic. He had hoped she wouldn't be disappointed with his choice of accommodations for their first weekend away together. Her reaction could have gone either way. Thankfully it was favorable, especially since he didn't have a backup plan.

With her arms full of their supplies for the weekend, Ilsa followed Dominic inside the cabin. It was dark inside, but as soon as the lights were turned on she got a good look at the place she'd call home for the next few days.

Placing everything on a small dining table, Dominic grabbed Ilsa's hand.

"Let me give you the grand tour," he said with a wide grin.

Without moving from where they were standing, he pointed to the left. "Living room slash family room. Kitchen and dining room," he said, gesturing toward the room they were in. Walking down the hall, he showed her the cabin's two bedrooms and one bathroom. "The room on the left is the master bedroom."

The term "master bedroom" seemed a bit of a stretch. The tiny room could barely accommodate the king-sized platform bed, a dresser pushed against one wall, and two small nightstands.

After the two of them finished unpacking the car and putting everything away, Ilsa turned and asked, "Now what?"

"Dinner," Dominic announced.

On the other side of the kitchen was a door that Ilsa soon discovered led out to a pretty impressive deck, complete with an outdoor sectional, grill, and fire pit.

"This little cabin has one surprise after another. From the front, you would never guess this deck was back here. Can we eat out here tonight?"

Happy to oblige, Dominic readily agreed. They gathered plates, cups, eating utensils, food, and a bottle of wine, and set up everything on the deck. To provide light and to keep bugs away, Dominic placed citronella candles along the deck's railing, adding the perfect backdrop to their outdoor dining experience.

Once they finished eating—a simple dinner of grilled hamburgers, corn on the cob, and a cucumber salad—they cleaned up and decided to stay outside to enjoy the late summer evening. In the background fireflies fluttered, crickets chirped, and a gentle wind rustled the leaves, reminding them that these types of evenings were to be savored.

"Come here."

Ilsa moved closer as the two of them snuggled in each other's arms.

"I'm glad you like it here. This is one of my favorite places to come and relax. Several years ago I bought this land with no particular purpose for it at the time but the price was right, and it seemed like a good investment. I somehow let a friend talk me into using it to build this cabin."

"How often do you come here?" Ilsa thought this was the kind of place that was perfect for getting away and unplugging.

"Not often enough."

Happy that Ilsa liked the cabin as much as he did, he decided right then that he would make an effort to spend more time here, with her.

"So what are we doing this weekend? Not that I would mind staying in this spot the entire time."

"Well, I want to take you into town and show you around. You can spend time there while I'm at work tomorrow or you can hang out here. I hate that you had to bring work with you this weekend, but I get it.

Hopefully, you'll be able to enjoy some downtime while I'm gone."

"I'll try." Dominic had no idea how much work she had to do, but he was right; she needed a break. She had already decided that she would complete what she could and not worry about anything that didn't get done.

"The weather is supposed to be nice tomorrow. Since I don't have to be at the restaurant until noon, we might get up early and go fishing. On Sunday, some of my friends are having a get-together, and I would love for you to meet them."

Meeting Dom's friends. Kind of an important step in their relationship, Ilsa thought. Other than Denita, Priscilla, and a few of her coworkers, Dominic hadn't met many of her other friends. They knew about him; they just hadn't met him yet. She needed to change that.

Ilsa wondered what kind of reception he would receive from her friends and family. In the back of her mind, she knew she would have to prepare her family to meet Dominic. Not that they would be shocked that she was in an interracial relationship, particularly since it seemed that Imani had dated guys from all over the globe, she simply wanted to avoid any awkwardness. *Something to think about later, not now.*

In the distance, a chorus of frogs sang out into the night as a cool breeze kicked up. As in most Midwestern states, it was getting to be the time of year when days were hot, but the nights could hold a bit of a chill. Ilsa rubbed her arms against the slight chill from the breeze.

"Cold?"

Dominic went inside and retrieved a chenille blanket. As they continued to listen to the night sounds without the distraction of traffic, TV, or other noises that didn't come from nature and snuggled under the warm blanket, Dominic savored every second. He couldn't put into words how he felt about having Ilsa all to himself for the entire weekend. The thought gave his spirit and his heart a lift.

Something had been absent from his life, and he hadn't even noticed—until now. Yet, he received a great deal of satisfaction from running his restaurant and everything involved with it. He also enjoyed an active social life and spending time with his family and friends. By most accounts, he had a pretty good life. But Ilsa had opened his eyes to another dimension, another way to view the world and his life with her in it. The funny thing is he didn't even know he was looking for her until she appeared. Now, the gradual realization that his life was indeed different dawned on him, and things would never be the same.

She probably had no idea how much joy, energy, and light she bought to his life, or how deeply he was falling in love.

CHAPTER TWENTY

"Rise and shine."

Startled awake by Dominic's greeting, Ilsa's pleasant dream abruptly ended. She had been dreaming about a place where she had a sense of absolute peace and serenity. The place was somewhere she'd never been, but she didn't feel odd being there. Instead, she felt loved, protected, and safe.

While her dream state had been nice, once conscious she remembered where she was and awakened with the same feeling of peace and serenity.

Last night had been wonderful. After staying out on the deck until very late—she had no idea of the time—they decided to get ready for bed. Once Dominic extinguished the fire in the fire pit, they cleaned up the dishes and tidied up. Afterward, they shared the tiny shower, lit candles in the tiny bathroom, and made love until they were completely spent and too exhausted to stay awake any longer.

Blinking to adjust to the light streaming into the room, Ilsa looked up to see Dominic standing next to the bed holding a cup. *How did he look so handsome and put together this early in the morning?*

"Good morning."

Sitting up on her elbows, she squinted. "Why are you up? I thought you didn't have to be at the restaurant until later."

"I thought we were going fishing," he said, handing her a cup of steaming hot coffee.

"Fishing? You were serious?"

Dominic laughed. "Yes, I was very serious. Come on. You'll love it. I promise. I have everything we need in the shed out back. I even got us some bait."

Ilsa groaned and took a tenuous sip of coffee. "You know, there are other things we can do for recreation, and we won't even have to leave this spot."

Catching the full meaning of her suggestion, Dominic quickly reconsidered. As much as he would have liked to stay in bed and make love to her all day, he also wanted to share with her some of the other things he loved. But the reality was that he knew the difficulty he would have leaving once he had Ilsa in his arms.

"I will hold you to that," he said, helping her out of bed. "Tonight, when we have more time, then I can be all yours. Now, get dressed. I made you some toast and a couple of boiled eggs."

Ilsa groaned even louder but dragged herself out of bed and to the bathroom. She looked at her reflection in the mirror. Her hair was everywhere. She typically tied her hair up at night with a scarf, but she had been too busy to worry about that last night.

After a quick shower, she slipped on a pair of jeans and t-shirt, joined Dominic at the table, and made quick work of her breakfast.

Once the kitchen was cleaned, Ilsa followed Dominic to the shed where they gathered the fishing equipment needed for their outing. He was right. He had everything they needed and then some.

"So, is there a spot you like best?" she asked as they walked side-by-side down a winding path leading to the lake.

Dominic stopped and grinned. "Yes, right here," he said, nuzzling her neck.

She made a face. "Oh no, I made that offer a little earlier and you shut me down."

"Don't hold that against me. You have no idea the effect you have on me. If I had taken you up on your offer, I wouldn't be any good the rest of the day, and

I need to be able to function at the restaurant today. I promise to make it up to you tonight."

"You'd better."

Once they found the perfect spot and set everything up, Dominic baited his hook and reached for Ilsa's to bait hers too.

She pulled away and grinned. "I can bait my own hook, thank you very much. My dad used to take me and my sisters fishing when we were kids."

"Okay, Miss Independent. Since you're an experienced angler, let's see how many fish you catch."

While they waited for their first bite, Ilsa broached the subject she had been thinking about since last night.

"What are your friends like? The ones I'm going to meet tomorrow."

Dominic recast his line. "They're nice people. I'm sure you'll like them."

"Will they like me?"

"Why wouldn't they?"

She fidgeted with her pole. "Do you think they'll be surprised by me?"

Dominic turned his attention from fishing to Ilsa. "Why would they?"

She looked worried. "Dom, some people aren't as accepting as we would like when it comes to interracial relationships."

"That's what you're worried about?"

"You're not?"

He laughed. "No, not at all. Any friend of mine who won't accept you or our relationship won't be a friend for long. Quite frankly, they probably weren't a true friend to begin with."

Content for now with his response, she dropped the subject and concentrated on catching more fish than Dominic.

However, after a morning spent without catching a single fish, Dominic and Ilsa headed back to the cabin so he could shower, change, and get ready to go back to the restaurant.

"What are you going to do while I'm gone?"

Ilsa was lying on the bed reading a book and glanced up just as Dominic emerged from the bathroom with a towel draped around his waist. Water glistened on his skin as he rummaged in the dresser drawer for something to wear.

Book forgotten, Ilsa quietly got out of bed and crept up behind him. With her fingertip, she traced a single drop of water as it traveled down his spine.

Surprised, Dominic turned around. Ilsa stood facing him wearing a smile so seductive he temporarily forgot about getting dressed and that he was supposed to head back to Columbus to get to work.

Within seconds they were in each other's arms as Dominic backed Ilsa toward the bed. On the way, she tripped. Falling back as she tried to regain her balance, she carried Dominic with her. Somewhere along the way, he lost the towel, saving her the effort of removing it.

With one hand, he caught her; with the other, he awkwardly braced himself to keep from landing on her with his full weight.

Not wasting one second of the few moments she managed to steal before he needed to leave, she lifted her mouth to his ear and whispered, "This is the appetizer for tonight."

At that moment, everything else was forgotten except the deep affection and fiery passion they shared.

CHAPTER TWENTY-ONE

"What do you think I should wear?"

Dominic shrugged and watched as Ilsa laid two different outfits across the bed. "I don't know. You know I like you in everything and when you're wearing absolutely nothing," he added with a wink.

Ilsa wanted to impress his friends, but she didn't want it to seem as if she was trying to impress them.

After watching her switch back and forth between the two outfits, Dominic tried to put her mind at ease. "This is a backyard barbecue. These are my friends. You have nothing to worry about. They are going to love you. Relax."

Settling on a simple summer dress, Ilsa decided to follow Dominic's advice. She felt a little silly for worrying about meeting his friends. She would be with him and everything would be fine.

When Dominic and Ilsa arrived at the party, it was already in full swing. Children were running and playing in one area of the yard, a small group of people played cards on the patio, and several men milled around the grill, presumably sharing grilling tips. People were everywhere, eating, drinking, laughing, and having a good time.

Dominic spotted a friend and took Ilsa by the hand so he could make introductions.

When Dominic's friend saw him approaching, he left the group of men he'd been talking with and met him. The two men exchanged "bro hugs" and slapped each other on the back.

Ilsa stood back as the two men greeted each other. She couldn't help smiling. In her experience, men weren't the most affectionate beings and often shied away from showing any type of warm feelings toward each other. Not in this case. She could tell this was a good friend of Dom's.

"Marshall Oliver. I'd like you to meet Ilsa Tanner."

Marshall smiled and took Ilsa's hand in a warm and firm handshake. "It's a pleasure to meet you, Ilsa." Turning his attention back to Dominic, he asked, "Have you introduced her to Trenay?"

"We just got here. You're our first stop."

"Take her around, Dom, and introduce her to everybody. Then come back and grab a beer so we can catch up."

Dominic did just that. When he rejoined Marshall, there was a cold beer waiting for him.

"Nice to see you could pull yourself away from the restaurant for a while."

"What can I say? Business has been good."

"Looks like something else is good," Marshall remarked, nodding toward Ilsa.

Dominic broke into a big grin. "I guess you could say that."

"You know I can't let it go unnoticed that this is the first woman you've ever bought to Benton Lake. I'm a little surprised you wanted to share your little hideaway with anybody. I'm guessing this is more than a casual thing."

Dominic took a swig of beer and nodded. "I certainly hope so."

While Dominic visited with his friend, Ilsa mingled with the other guests. She met so many people at the party she couldn't keep up with all of the names or relationships, although she did learn that Marshall and his brother Lee were close friends of Dom's. She could tell he wanted to spend some male bonding time with them so she shooed him off while she made conversation with a couple who ran the town's farmer's market.

The couple was as nice as could be and told Ilsa all about the advantages of living in a small town. Admittedly, she only half-listened as she watched Dominic talking and joking around with Lee and Marshall. Nothing about this man was lost on her, from his mannerisms to his sheer masculinity and everything in between.

From time to time Dominic looked over at Ilsa to make sure she was enjoying herself, but he didn't want to leave her alone for too long. Stepping away from his friends after a while, he joined her just as she was being given the rundown on the benefits of living on a farm.

"Excuse me, but I need to steal this pretty lady for a few minutes."

Ilsa left the farmer's market couple with a promise to visit their market before she left town.

"Having fun?"

She nodded. "Yes, there are so many interesting people here. I met a woman who owns a coffee shop and bookstore. Sounds like the type of place I could lose myself in."

"That would be Katrice. She's Lee's wife."

"Oh. I should have made the connection. Lots of people, lots of dots to connect. How exactly do you know all these people? Have you lived here before?"

Taking a sip of beer, Dominic shook his head. "I know it seems like I do, but I really don't know everyone here. Quite a few folks, though. Lee used to live in Columbus and does some legal work for me from time to time. Marshall owns the company that built my cabin at the lake. I've met a lot of people through them. I also meet people when I come here to fish and spend time at the cabin."

Ilsa let that bit of information sink in for a second. Lee and Marshall were Black. So not only did Dominic have a Black attorney, but he also used a minority-owned company to build his cabin. He had once told her that he did not choose his friends or colleagues based on color but on their character and the ability to be true to their word.

Ilsa leaned up and placed a kiss on Dominic's cheek.

"What was that for?" he asked, smiling.

"That's for being an amazing man and a pretty cool human."

As the party came to a close, Ilsa and Dominic said their goodbyes. She heard Dominic promise to spend more time with Lee and Marshall the next time he was in town.

Ilsa had met both men's wives and clicked with them. She, too, wouldn't mind spending more time with them and hoped they would have an opportunity to all do something together soon.

Driving back to the cabin, Ilsa and Dominic shared a comfortable silence. Ilsa thought about the wonderful time she'd had over the weekend and tried not to focus on having to leave the next day. She liked and would miss exploring the woods around the cabin, their quiet evenings spent on the deck, and, even though she'd sucked at it, fishing with Dominic.

She didn't mind the quietness in the car. Talking or not talking, it didn't matter. It was equally good. They would have to make time to come back before too much time passed.

At first, she had been a little nervous with the idea of spending this much time alone with Dominic, but the weekend had proven to be beneficial to their relationship. She loved meeting his friends, being at the cabin—one of his favorite places to relax and unwind—and even spending time doing routine things like cooking, gathering wood for the fire pit, and buying groceries. Something about being with Dominic felt comfortable, exciting, and right. He was easy to talk to, and they talked about everything from current events to family drama, work, cars, sports, and life in general.

Dominic was a good listener. At times she felt guilty when she unloaded about everything going on at her job, but he didn't seem to mind and had quickly learned the difference between the times she needed to vent and when she simply wanted advice. It meant a lot to her that he could tell the difference.

And there was something else—something she didn't want to spend too much time analyzing but thought about nonetheless; she was quickly learning how deeply Dominic cared for her. The looks, the touches, the little things he did for her just because, and the way he let her know she was a priority in his life. All of this made her feel special, appreciated, and cared for.

She didn't need to wonder where their relationship was headed. The specifics weren't important at the moment. Enjoying what they had and being in the moment was the only thing she cared about.

Dominic didn't mind the quiet drive back to the cabin either. Thinking about their weekend and how much he enjoyed being with Ilsa kept his mind busy. Bringing her to the lake had been a gamble. She would have either liked the rustic setting and no-frills cabin or she wouldn't have. He was grateful and relieved she did—very much, it seemed.

There was so much about this woman he adored. He liked surprising her and sharing his world with her. He truly enjoyed getting to know her on a level he'd never experienced with another woman.

What he had learned was that at times she could be vulnerable but never a pushover; other times she could be an immovable force. Her compassion for the women she served at New Hope was more than a job to her; this was how she lived her life—with passion, sincerity, and being one hundred percent present.

He knew she had been nervous about meeting his friends. It was sweet that she cared enough to want to make a good impression. And she had. He'd caught glimpses of her interacting with people at the party and all he could think was, *This beautiful, funny, and amazing woman is here with me!*

He thought about their relationship and where it was headed. In his mind, they had all the time in the world to do whatever they wanted, but his heart no longer wanted to simply do *whatever.* For the first time in a long time, he no longer thought in terms of just himself. Now he thought of himself *with* Ilsa. And that, in his book, was a very good thing.

CHAPTER TWENTY-TWO

The weeks after returning from Benton Lake were busy for both Dominic and Ilsa. The restaurant had been extremely busy. With Lu away on vacation, Dominic couldn't spend as much time with Ilsa as he would have liked. Even their Thursday date nights had been put on a temporary hiatus. Fortunately, Lu would be back before his mother arrived, so he would be able to enjoy her visit.

Ilsa had been busy too. Grant had made several nearly impossible demands that required everyone to spend a lot of time revamping the center's processes and reassigning workloads. And with the recent resignations, they each had to pitch in to fill in the gap. Ilsa had wanted to go home to visit her parents, but with the amount of extra work that needed to be done, she had to postpone her trip.

Regardless of their work demands, whatever time Dominic and Ilsa managed to spend with each other, they took full advantage. Typically they would either meet at Ilsa's late at night after Dominic left the restaurant or she would wait for him at his loft. Neither of them minded the lack of sleep, unorthodox meal times, where they met, or even the day of the week. They simply wanted to be together.

The Monday before Dominic's mother was scheduled to arrive, Ilsa went to his loft to help prepare for her visit. She loved his loft. He told her he had purchased the abandoned building several years earlier at an auction. Seeing potential in the old warehouse where no one else had, the investment eventually paid off handsomely. Turning the space into several loft-style apartments, he rented out the other units and kept the largest one, on the top floor, for himself. The wide-open space with a few sectioned private areas had a special charm and character that fit Dominic's personality.

Ilsa loved the exposed brick, hardwood floors, gourmet kitchen, and floor-to-ceiling windows that took up three of the four walls. What she didn't like were the bare windows. It shouldn't have mattered that much since they were on the third floor, but she couldn't help feeling exposed to the outside world. No curtains or blinds meant no privacy, something that escaped Dominic and didn't appear to bother him one bit.

Ilsa helped ready the guestroom and spruce up the rest of Dominic's space which, despite all of its charm, in her opinion, couldn't be more "male." It was void of the kind of touches that made a house a home. Ilsa brought over a few things from her house and purchased a couple of items from one of her favorite shops that she thought might soften things up a bit and make the space cozier. Candles, a colorful throw for the sofa, and a set of lamps that bought more subtle lighting into the open living room were just a few added touches. On a whim, and because she loved green things growing indoors, she found a plant that looked great near the windows in the kitchen. Giving explicit instructions to Dominic on its care and survival, she made a mental note to keep tabs on the plant herself.

Once finished and satisfied with their work, they took a break to appreciate everything they had accomplished. Ilsa lit one of the candles she had purchased from her lotions and potions supplier, as Dominic referred to her, and joined him on the sofa. The scent of vanilla filled the air. Inside, everything was perfect. Outside, Ilsa could hear the beginnings of a storm as raindrops hit against the windows.

"Thank you for helping me with all of this."

She snuggled against him. "I didn't mind at all. I've been dying to add some softer touches to this place. This was my opportunity and I wasn't going to miss it."

Dominic laughed. "Are you trying to change me?"

"Not at all. I like that you're a little rough around the edges. I just thought the place could use a little more softness and charm and a bit less testosterone and man cave."

"I guess you're right. Overall, I like what you've done, except for the plant. I can't promise it'll still be alive the next time you come over."

It began to rain harder. Not long after, lightning lit up the night sky followed by loud crashes of thunder.

Dominic turned off the lamps, leaving the only light in the room emitting from the single candle and the occasional bolt of lightning.

"By the way, I will probably never light those candles when you're not here."

"Why not? Don't you like them?"

"I only like them with you."

As the rain continued to beat against the windows, the thunder and lightning added the backdrop for a perfect romantic evening. Ilsa felt more happy and content than she had in a long time. Once again, she thought about how nice it was to spend time with Dominic. Like before, she thought about how it felt good sharing even the simplest of tasks.

Earlier she had talked to Dominic about being anxious to meet his mother. He had assured her the two of them would hit it off and she had nothing to worry about. She decided he was probably right. After all, how could someone who'd raised such a wonderful man like Dominic be at all bad?

"Do you want me to go with you to pick up your mother from the airport on Wednesday?"

"No, she decided to take an earlier flight and should be here about two-ish. I don't want you to have to take off from work, but I do want to make sure you'll be here Thursday evening for dinner."

"I wouldn't miss it for the world."

It didn't seem as if the storm would be letting up anytime soon, but stormy weather or not, it didn't matter. Neither Ilsa nor Dominic wanted to be anywhere else.

Marta's plane arrived on time. While Dominic waited for her to deplane, he sent Ilsa a text.

You've been on my mind all day. Can't wait to see you tomorrow night. Wear something sexy. He added an emoji with googly eyes.

As the crowds began to increase, Dominic looked for his mother amongst the travelers. Finally spotting her, he hurried forward, enveloping her in a big hug.

"Mom, it's good to see you." He hadn't realized how much he'd missed her. It had been less than a year since her last visit, but in that time it seemed as if she'd aged a little more than he remembered. *Maybe it was fatigue from traveling*, he reasoned.

"Dominic, look at you! My beautiful boy," she exclaimed, happy to see her son whom she missed terribly.

"Come on. Let's get your luggage."

On the drive home, Dominic listened as his mother told him about the woman she'd sat beside on the plane. She was new to the city, having recently been transferred by her job. Marta told her all about her son's restaurant and also gave her recommendations for places to meet people so she wouldn't feel so alone in her new hometown.

Dominic found his mother's advice funny and interesting all at the same time. Funny, because it had been years since his mother lived in the area, and here she was giving advice about places to meet people. And interesting, because most of the places she mentioned were still good places for just that.

"I need to go to the restaurant for a little while. Do you want to go with me or should I take you home so you can unpack and rest?"

As much as she loved spending time at her son's restaurant, the trip had tired her out a little more than she had expected. "I think I'll be much better company after I've rested a bit. By the way, is Ilsa coming over tonight so I can meet her or will I have to wait until dinner tomorrow?"

"Tomorrow."

"I can hardly wait to meet her, Dom. Remember, I'm doing all the cooking for dinner tomorrow."

"Mom, I want to tell you something about Ilsa before you meet her."

"Yes?"

"Do you remember when I first told you about her? You asked if she was Greek or Italian."

"Yes."

"I told you she's neither. She's Black."

Dominic waited to let the news sink in. He had already prepared himself for a variety of responses, and while he had told Ilsa she had nothing to worry about when meeting his mother, he wasn't one hundred percent sure himself. He didn't know how she would react because, quite frankly, he hadn't been serious enough with anyone, other than his ex-wife, long enough to want to introduce them to his family. His mother never knew any of the women he'd dated.

Dominic pulled into his assigned parking space and turned off the engine.

"Well?"

Marta turned to her son and asked, "Is she a nice person, Dom?"

"Of course."

"Does she make you happy?"

He nodded and swallowed a lump in his throat. "Yes, Mom, she makes me very happy."

"Sweetheart, I am an old woman."

Dominic started to interrupt, but Marta stopped him. "I learned a long time ago to open my mind and heart to all people. As a result, I have friendships that I wouldn't trade for anything in this world. I wasn't always this open, and for that I have regrets. I'm glad that you are wiser than I ever was. The only things your father and I ever wanted for you and your sister were for you to be happy, safe, successful, and loved. When you talk about Ilsa, I listen to your words, and I also hear what's in your heart. It's your heart that tells me you love this woman even if you have yet to put your feelings into words. From what you've told me, I would venture to say she feels the same about you. And that is more than good enough for me."

CHAPTER TWENTY-THREE

Ilsa gripped the steering wheel, quietly fuming as she sat in bumper-to-bumper traffic. If she could get away with it, she'd wring Grant's neck. He knew she had plans to leave early, but at the last minute he called her into his office with a request for a report that anyone with a fifth-grade knowledge of spreadsheets would have been able to produce—anyone except Grant.

The man was beyond inept. She had lost track of the number of times she showed him where the reports were saved and even how to access them. Every time she had to repeat the same information over and over left her mentally exhausted and questioning how anyone thought he was the right person for the director's job.

Now because of his last-minute request, she would have to move at super-speed to make it to Dominic's on time. It was a good thing she planned ahead and had the outfit she was going to wear laid out on her bed. A quick shower, change, and a little makeup shouldn't take her more than forty-five minutes. She even remembered Dom's text to wear something sexy, although she would be wearing something more meet-the-mother appropriate: a royal blue knit dress with gold accent buttons. Not over the top, the dress complimented her skin tone and showed off her curves while revealing just a tiny bit of cleavage. For fun, she slipped on a lacy bra and panty set in the same color blue.

Ilsa stood outside Dominic's door, took a deep breath, and rang the doorbell. Opening the door to greet her, he did a quick head-to-toe perusal, winked, and nodded in appreciation before giving her a quick kiss on the lips.

"Why didn't you use your key?" he whispered.

"Because I didn't want your mother to know I had one," she whispered back.

Amused, he reminded her, "We're adults."

"She's still your mother, and I want to make a good first impression."

Holding Dominic's hand as he led her to the kitchen, Ilsa saw his mother standing over the stove vigorously stirring something in a large pan.

"Mom," Dominic called out. "She's here."

Marta looked up from the steaming pot, wiped her hands on her apron, and smiled broadly.

Ilsa stepped forward and extended her hand, but Marta opened her arms and wrapped her in a tight hug instead.

Stepping back, she took Ilsa's hands into hers and looked up at her with the same sparkling dark eyes as Dominic's. "I can see why my Dom is smitten with you. You're beautiful."

Ilsa smiled as relief washed over her. Marta's words and gestures seemed and felt very genuine. "Thank you," she replied. "It smells amazing in here. I can hardly wait for dinner."

"It won't be much longer. I hope you're hungry."

After exchanging pleasantries, Marta shooed Dominic and Ilsa out of the kitchen so she could finish preparing the meal. She refused all offers of help and appeared to be in her element as she puttered around in the kitchen.

Sitting on the sofa with Dominic, Ilsa could tell he was happy to have his mother here.

"Feel better?" he asked.

"Yes," she replied, taking a sip of the wine he had waiting for her on the coffee table. "I just wanted to be prepared in case..."

"In case she didn't accept you?"

Ilsa nodded.

"Dinner's ready," Marta announced.

Marta outdid herself preparing an excellent meal. Dominic had previously told her he named his restaurant, YiaYia's Table, after his *yiayia*, his grandmother. He was also quick to give credit to his mother from whom he had learned a great deal about cooking and who was a phenomenal cook in her own right.

Beginning with a warm bacon, sautéed mushroom, and arugula salad, Marta then served roasted pork loin cooked over cabbage with a white wine and dried cherry sauce. There was even freshly baked bread. And for dessert, there was a simple but exquisite roasted pear, blueberry, and grape compote complete with a cookie.

"Mrs. Markos, everything is delicious. I don't know if I'll be able to eat anything else for the next few days."

"Please, call me Marta. And thank you. I'm glad you're enjoying your meal."

"Mom's been cooking all day. She wouldn't even allow me in the kitchen."

"Good food takes time to prepare, and I wanted to make something different and delicious for tonight. Besides, I don't have many opportunities to cook like this anymore. Sometimes I miss it."

"Does your church still provide free meals on Saturdays?" Dominic asked.

Marta nodded. "We do, but that's different. Those are usually simple meals." She turned to Ilsa to explain. "Every Saturday, my church provides meals to anyone in the community who needs food and companionship."

"Companionship?" Ilsa asked.

"Yes," Marta replied. "It's sad, but you would be surprised by the number of people who don't have anyone to talk to regularly or who have no one to check on them. I think we have just as many people coming to the Saturday meal out of the need for companionship as those who simply don't have enough food to eat at home. In this digital world, we tend to forget the importance of real human interaction. For people who live alone or who are housebound, that interaction is vitally important. We do our best to fill both needs."

After they finished eating, Dominic insisted on clearing the dishes himself and putting the food away. He whisked Ilsa and his mother off to the living room. Purposely taking his time cleaning up in the kitchen, he wanted to give the two of them ample time to talk and get to know each other.

The two women chatted while Dominic worked in the kitchen. Marta talked about current events, food, family, and shared little details about her life. Ilsa was surprised to learn that in addition to Marta's work at her church, she also volunteered as a reading buddy at a local elementary school. She provided tutoring to children who struggled with reading.

Ilsa talked about her work at New Hope, her two boys, new daughter-in-law, and her family in Cincinnati. She mentioned the volunteer work her mother was involved in and how her father joked her mother was busier now than she ever was when she was working a full-time job.

Marta also told Ilsa about her recent trip to see her daughter and her family in California. She had a special gleam in her eye when she talked about her grandchildren.

"Does anyone want coffee?"

Both women declined.

"It's much too late for me to have caffeine," Marta said, stifling a yawn. "In fact, I think it's time for me to turn in for the evening."

Marta rose to leave but turned to Ilsa. "Good night, dear. I do hope we get to spend a little more time together before I go back to Arizona."

Ilsa stood and hugged Marta. "I would like that very much."

After his mother left, Dominic lit some of the candles Ilsa had previously brought over. Then he turned on some music. Standing in the middle of the floor, he held out his hand, beckoning her to join him.

Ilsa looked toward his mother's room and gave him a questioning look.

"Come on, I want to dance with you. My mom is worn out from cooking all day. In a few minutes, she'll be fast asleep and won't even know we're here."

Ilsa walked across the room and into Dominic's waiting arms.

"You made my mother very happy tonight."

"No, I think it was the other way around. Your mother made *me* very happy tonight, about ten pounds worth. I can't remember the last time I had homemade bread. This is going to require a lot of extra time at the gym."

Dominic pulled Ilsa in closer. "By the way, I forgot to tell you how pretty you look tonight. I love the dress. Blue is definitely your color. Oh, and I love your latest combination of smells."

Ilsa giggled. He had such a way with words. "I thought you might."

"I'm serious about what I said a few minutes ago. My mother was excited about meeting you and spending time with you this evening."

"Me too. She's a nice lady. There was no reason for me to be nervous at all."

Ilsa rested her head against Dominic's chest. His arm, wrapped around her body, kept her close as they danced slowly to a hauntingly romantic song. The artist was a local singer they'd heard during a summer concert they had attended on one of their Thursday dates. The singer's voice, low and throaty, sang of a love for all seasons.

The first time we met, it was a summer's eve.

I saw your face and for a moment had a reprieve.

When we marveled at the colors that painted the fall

I no longer asked of life, is this it? Is this all?

Grateful the bitter winds of winter no longer touched my soul.

Your love protects me, you've made me whole.

Now I am free to love and to accept the offerings of life.

In the springtime, I said yes to be your wife.

Dominic's hand rested gently on Ilsa's back. He leaned down and kissed her forehead. She closed her eyes and snuggled in closer.

Dominic wished he could stop time, making this moment last forever. Ilsa had no idea how happy she made him. Every time they were together, it got better and better. How could he be this lucky to have this wonderful, beautiful, and perfect woman in his life? What would his life be without her? Truthfully, he didn't want to know, especially now that he knew what his life was like with her in it. He couldn't imagine it any other way.

He couldn't help wondering, did she feel the same about him? They hadn't talked about their feelings or their relationship in general. But maybe it was time.

"Ilsa?"

"Yes?"

"I have something I need to tell you."

"Okay," she said quietly.

"I love you."

CHAPTER TWENTY-FOUR

He loves me. "He loves me," Ilsa said aloud. Dominic's words still echoed in her mind, but now some of the surprise had worn off.

Why did this catch her so off guard? They hadn't talked about their feelings before now. The topic hadn't come up, and there had been no pressing reason to bring it up.

She cared for Dominic deeply, but love? Maybe what they were feeling was misguided lust, she rationalized. Maybe infatuation or comfortable companionship. Seriously, had there been enough time to fall in love? Was it even love?

Dominic had called and left messages, but she had been too busy to talk, or so she'd said. Honestly, she didn't know what to say to him. That night—the night he had shared his feelings—she had frozen and, in a panic, made up an excuse about needing to get home to finish something for work. In what seemed like seconds she grabbed her coat and purse and left abruptly, all in that order.

How could three little words throw her whole psyche into such a tailspin?

Realistically, she couldn't avoid Dominic forever, nor did she want to. She simply needed a little time to come to terms with the fact that this man just confessed his love for her and she didn't know what to do about it.

Fortunately, she had a little time to sort through it all. Dominic had taken his mother to Amish country for the day and would be spending the evening at the restaurant. Lu had a bad cold and wouldn't be able to cover for him over the weekend, so he would be tied up then too. Dominic didn't want to leave his mother alone for the weekend, she learned from a voicemail message. He asked if she wouldn't mind coming by and spending some time with her. She replied, via text, agreeing to take her shopping or to the movies. Truthfully, she was happy to do it and didn't mind spending more time getting to know more about Marta. There were plenty of things they could do together while also buying a little time to allow her to get her head and heart straight before facing Dominic.

Mid-morning on Saturday, Ilsa showed up to get Marta after Dominic had already left for work, something she had intentionally planned.

Ilsa learned that Marta liked antiquing, so the two women set out on a treasure hunt. She only knew of three shops in town, but Marta knew a few others. They spent the morning browsing through other people's long forgotten and discarded treasures, occasionally finding a few knickknacks that were worth buying.

The evaluation of trinkets and the process of browsing through items took longer than Ilsa had anticipated, but she didn't mind. She hadn't made any other plans for the day and shopping proved to be an effective distraction.

As they talked about where to have lunch, Ilsa prayed Marta wouldn't suggest Dominic's restaurant. Thankfully, she didn't. Instead, she suggested a small diner she liked to frequent when she came to town.

"This is fun. I haven't been to an antique shop in years. I'd forgotten about all of the cool things there are to find in these places."

Marta agreed. "Too many tempting treasures to pass up. I know I don't need to buy anything, but I couldn't resist that little yellow teapot."

The two women ordered lunch and made plans to visit a few other stores that afternoon. After finishing their entrees, they agreed to extend lunch a little longer with coffee and dessert before heading back out into the crisp autumn air.

"I am thoroughly enjoying my visit with Dominic," Marta said, "and meeting and spending time with you."

Ilsa smiled. She genuinely liked Marta and enjoyed spending time with her as well. "I'm glad you were able to come out for a visit. It means a lot to Dom to have you here, and it also means a lot to me."

"Do you mind if I ask you a question?"

"No, not at all."

"Did something happen between you and Dom the other night?"

About to take a sip of coffee, Ilsa stopped halfway to her mouth. She placed the cup back on its saucer. "Why? Did Dominic say something?" She held her breath. Was their lovely lunch about to take an intrusive turn? She hoped Marta wasn't going to turn into one of those mothers who inserted themselves into their adult children's personal lives.

Marta smiled knowingly. "He didn't have to."

Okay, maybe she had incorrectly made a snap judgment. Ilsa sighed. Unsure of how much she could and should share, she hesitated before responding. "We just have a few things to talk through. That's all."

Marta nodded. "My son," she began, only hesitating momentarily as she reminded herself not to overstep her boundaries, "is not a complicated man. He says what he means and he means what he says. He is also not good at hiding his feelings, never has been. So when you came to dinner the other night, I saw the way he looked at you, how he spoke to you, and even before that, how he spoke about you. It wasn't hard to figure out his true feelings for you."

Understanding what Marta implied, she asked, "You know?"

"Yes, I know that my son loves you."

"Did he tell you that? Did he say those exact words?"

Marta smiled and waved her hand dismissively. "He didn't have to."

"Marta, I have to be honest with you and myself. I don't know if I'm ready for love and all the compromises, requirements, and crazy ups and downs that are attached to it. Don't get me wrong, I care for Dominic very deeply. And believe me, my feelings toward him have also taken me by surprise. Part of me wants to slow down and take things one day at a time. Another part reminds me that life is short, and you have to grab happiness and joy where you can and while you can."

"Care for a piece of advice from an old lady?"

Ilsa peered across the table at Marta and wrinkled her brow. "You're not old."

"Tell that to my joints," Marta joked.

"What advice do you have for me? I think I could use some about now."

"You are absolutely correct. Life is short and it's important to grab happiness and joy when it's within your grasp, but in the process don't run away from it or try to analyze it to death. That will most certainly lead to confusion and conflicted emotions. One important thing I've learned is that sometimes it's okay to be led by your heart and not your brain. Another thing I've learned is that it doesn't take a lifetime to know when something is right and good and special. If you don't mind me saying so, I think what you and Dom have is all of those things."

After their interesting and insightful talk at lunch and spending the remainder of the afternoon treasure hunting, Ilsa dropped Marta off at the loft with her bags and boxes of special finds. It had been a day filled with adventure, discovery, and negotiating. She had thoroughly enjoyed herself and had developed a newfound respect for Marta's ability to sniff out unique finds and negotiate killer deals. Most of all, she had appreciated her talk with Marta about what was going on between her and Dominic.

After all, what was she afraid of? Love wasn't supposed to be scary.

She needed to sort through her jumbled feelings, and the sooner the better. Avoiding Dominic wouldn't be something she could do forever, nor would she be able to.

CHAPTER TWENTY-FIVE

Denita and her husband were surprised to hear the doorbell since they weren't expecting company. When Cam opened the door and saw Ilsa, the look on her face told him everything he needed to know. She needed Denita. Having been a party to his wife and Ilsa's friendship all these years, he had learned to read all the looks. Joy, excitement, sadness, fear—he couldn't begin to guess which one this was. But he knew enough to not waste time with small talk.

"Denita, baby, Ilsa's here."

Ilsa stepped inside and patted Cam on the arm, thankful for his understanding and willingness to share his wife with her.

Denita stepped out of the family room, took one look at her friend, and said, "This must be serious for you to show up at nine-forty-five on a Saturday night."

"Serious enough."

Cam had since disappeared to another part of the house, leaving the two women alone to work through whatever it was they needed to work through.

Ilsa tossed her coat onto a nearby chair in the family room and sat down in one of the big, comfy, overstuffed chairs across from the sofa. Denita sat on the sofa waiting patiently to find out what had her friend in such a funk.

"Want a glass of wine?"

Ilsa shook her head.

"Chocolate?"

"No."

"Coffee or tea?"

"No, I don't want anything. I just need to talk."

Denita settled back onto the couch and covered up with a fluffy throw. "Okay, I'm listening."

"I finally got to meet Dom's mother. Remember I told you she was going to be in town this week?"

Denita nodded.

"Well, Dom had me over for dinner on Thursday. Marta, Dominic's mother, made a killer meal." Ilsa went on to describe the meal, right down to the dessert. "She's a very good cook. We even had homemade bread, which I ate way too much of."

Denita continued to listen while she waited patiently for Ilsa to stop talking about what she'd eaten for dinner and get to the point.

"Everything was perfect, Dee. The meal, the conversation, everything. Then Dom's mother goes to bed and leaves us alone. We're talking, listening to music, dancing-"

"Dancing?"

Ilsa smiled, remembering that part of the evening. "Yeah, that's kind of our thing sometimes."

"And then what? Or do I want to know?"

"You want to know. When we were dancing, Dom must have gotten caught up in the moment or had too much wine and he said something I wasn't expecting."

Concerned, Denita wondered aloud what he could have said that was so unexpected and serious.

"He said he loved me."

Sitting up, Denita let out a little scream. "What? Really? He said the L-word? Wow! That's great!" But when she looked at Ilsa who wasn't exhibiting the same level of excitement, she was confused. "Uh, Ilsa, am I missing something? The man said he loves you. We, or you, should be happy about that, right?"

"I didn't say it back. Actually, not only did I not say it, I made up some stupid excuse about having to finish something for work, and I grabbed my stuff and bolted.

It's weird, but I felt like I needed to get out of there as fast as I could. And I did."

"Why?"

Ilsa threw her hands up. "I don't know. Sadly, that was my first reaction; I didn't say it was the right one."

"What did he say after that? Is he hurt? I'm pretty sure he's confused."

"Well, I've been avoiding him, so I don't know what he's feeling."

"Wait, wait, wait, Ilsa. This isn't adding up. What's really going on? You're crazy about Dominic. Why didn't you tell him that?"

"Because I'm an idiot."

Denita leaned forward, looked her friend directly in the eye, and said, "No, you're not an idiot. You heard love and you panicked."

"Maybe."

"Not maybe, definitely. The reality is that you haven't loved another man since Quinn. And I'd be willing to bet you didn't plan on loving anyone else either. Then here comes Dominic with his good looks, charm, picnics, and dancing, and he showers you with some much-needed attention and affection. I'm pretty sure with your 'take one day at a time' attitude, feelings were growing stronger right before your eyes, or heart in this case, and you never gave it much thought. You didn't know what hit you with that man, did you?"

Ilsa shook her head. Denita was more correct than she knew.

"So I bet you've been thinking about the situation, and you've been analyzing it to death, right? Looking at it from different angles and picking apart every reason why he fell in love with you and what you're supposed to do about it. 'Is it too soon? Is it really love? Blah, blah, blah.'"

"You do know me, don't you?"

"Like the back of my hand."

"I just want to know one thing; do you love him, Ilsa?"

Ilsa took in a deep breath and let it out slowly. "I think I do, Dee. I wasn't ready to admit it before. Maybe because I thought I was giving up something by admitting it or committing to something I didn't think I was ready for, but I do think I love him. It's still kind of scary acknowledging it, but at the same time it feels good."

"Good. I'm glad we got to the bottom of that. Now you need to tell him."

"I would, but, unfortunately, I think I've made a big mess of everything."

"Then fix it."

A sound piece of advice, Ilsa thought. If only it were that easy.

CHAPTER TWENTY-SIX

It was late when Ilsa turned down her street heading home. The conversation with Denita still fresh, she was grateful to have someone rational and understanding to talk to about her feelings. Wondering how much she had messed things up between her and Dominic, she knew it would be up to her to fix things.

What did she have to be afraid of? Why was she having such a hard time telling Dominic how she felt? Men were the ones who supposedly had a hard time expressing their feelings, not women.

Dominic had called several times over the past few days and sent multiple text messages, only a few of which she returned. Having no idea if he was upset, confused, or hurt made her feel guilty, but she needed a little while longer to figure out what she wanted to say and how she planned to apologize. She would get a good night's sleep and put a plan into place tomorrow.

Ilsa tossed her keys on the table and hung her purse on the back of a chair. It was late and she felt drained, both mentally and physically. The only thing she had the energy for was a hot shower and bed. On her way up the stairs to her bedroom, the sound of the doorbell stopped her. Checking the time on her cell phone, she thought it was much too late for a casual visitor.

Standing at the front door, she asked, "Who is it?"

"Ilsa, it's me."

Dominic. She needed more time to think about what she wanted to say. After ignoring him for days, how was she going to say what she needed to without thinking it through first? So much for formulating a plan. *Time to face the music.* Reluctantly, she opened the door.

"We need to talk." Dispensing with all pleasantries, Dominic walked right in.

"It's late."

Ignoring her half-hearted protest, he turned to Ilsa.

His eyes reflected an emotion she had never seen. Anger? Hurt?

"You've been avoiding me, and I need to know why."

He sounded angry. Unprepared to have this conversation, she fumbled for the right words. "I don't know how to explain it. Everything I want to say just doesn't seem right."

"Explain what? Why you ran away when I told you I loved you? Why you've been ignoring me when you know I've been trying to talk to you? Why you can't bring yourself to tell me you love me too?"

Now Ilsa was annoyed. "Sounds like I don't need to explain anything. Sounds like you have all the answers."

Dominic softened his tone. He didn't want to fight. That's not why he showed up at her house unannounced. "Talk to me. Tell me what's going on. Are you afraid of loving me, Ilsa?"

For the first time that evening, Ilsa looked at Dominic, really looked at him. Where she thought she would see anger, she saw love. Where there should have been confusion, she saw understanding. And because of what she saw, she felt she could finally say what was in her heart.

"Yes, Dom, I did run away for all the reasons you said. At first, I didn't know why, but when I confronted my feelings, I knew the reason. I panicked. Plain and simple. Things between us have moved so effortlessly that I didn't recognize what was happening between us or even how deep our feelings were becoming." Frustrated that she wasn't saying exactly what she felt, she tried another approach. "Of course, I realized that our feelings for each other were changing and growing stronger, but love? You have to admit, love can be a pretty scary word sometimes."

"It doesn't have to be."

She nodded. "That's what I keep telling myself."

"Then what are you afraid of?"

She shrugged. "The unknown, I guess. I haven't been serious about or shared this much of my life with anyone since my husband, and even now, all of this is very different."

"Look, the last thing in the world I ever wanted to do was to overwhelm or pressure you. I'm so sorry if I did." Dominic walked toward her. Taking her face between his hands, he kissed her forehead, her eyelids, and then her lips before letting go. "The one thing I don't regret is telling you how I feel. I'm crazy about you, Ilsa. I don't see that changing any time soon, no matter how much you try to avoid me. There is no one I'd rather sit up all night hammering through spreadsheets with or cuddling up with during a storm. And don't even think about going fishing without me. Face it, you're stuck with me."

She smiled. Looking into Dominic's eyes, she felt her fears slowly melting away. This man loved her. She had no reason to fear that. Everything between them had been good to this point. Why wouldn't it continue to be? She remembered Marta's advice from their earlier conversation. *Sometimes it's okay to be led by your heart, not your brain.*

Maybe it was okay after all to follow her heart this time. She had been avoiding Dominic for the past several days. She now realized just how much she missed him. It was time—time to tell him what was in her heart and what she had been afraid to admit. Gone was the anxiety and the need for hesitation. Her heart and head were in synch.

"You know, something you said earlier was actually correct."

"Really? What was it?"

"I do love you."

CHAPTER TWENTY-SEVEN

It had been a nice week. Grant was out of the office doing God knows what practically every day, and the staff truly appreciated his absence. Ilsa and Dominic were back in synch and had spent a few evenings alone together and even some time together with Marta. One night they all attended a local production of *Cats*. On another, Ilsa had Dominic and his mother to her house for dinner.

Now all she wanted was to get started on her weekend. Before shutting everything down, she called to check on Tia. She got her voicemail and left a message stating that she was thinking about her and wanted to make sure she was doing okay. Ilsa also asked her to call back and let her know how her computer classes were going.

After sending replies to a few emails and scheduling a meeting with Priscilla to review paperwork for a grant, she was finally ready to shut down her computer and get ready to leave.

"Heading out?" Priscilla stuck her head in the door, bundling up against the cold autumn air as she, too, prepared to leave.

"Yes, ma'am. Give me a second, and I'll walk out with you."

Just as she was buttoning her coat, her desk phone rang. Looking at the caller ID, she saw Grant's extension displayed on the small screen.

"I thought Grant had already left for the day."

Priscilla shrugged. "I guess he slithered back in."

Ilsa took a deep breath and answered the call. "Yes, Grant. How can I help you?"

After a few seconds, Ilsa placed the receiver back on the cradle. "Go ahead. This may take a while."

As much as she liked and respected Ilsa, Priscilla had no desire to wait around at work any longer than was necessary.

Ilsa stepped into Grant's office wearing her game face, mentally prepared for whatever was about to be thrown her way. She stood in front of his desk as he typed something into his computer. She continued to wait patiently for him to finish as she fought to keep from being annoyed that he was making her wait.

"Sorry about that," he said. "I just needed to send off a reply to an email before I forgot."

Grant picked up a memo from his desk, glanced over it, and put it in his desk drawer. Again, Ilsa patiently waited for him to tell her why he had called her into his office.

"I've been looking over the activities and budget for the staff appreciation day."

"Yes, it's a great morale booster for the staff and lets them know how much they are appreciated. Everyone looks forward to it." *Please don't tell me you're going to attend.*

"I'm afraid we're going to have to cut back this year. I've made some adjustments to the budget and reallocated some of the funds."

Grant handed Ilsa a piece of paper.

Scanning the document, she couldn't believe what she was seeing. Attempting to tamp down her rising anger, she looked at the final figure, and then at Grant, who she could have sworn was smirking. "Grant, this isn't enough to buy cheese and crackers, let alone lunch for twenty-plus people."

Grant shrugged nonchalantly. "We need to cut back on expenses and since this activity doesn't directly impact the clients, it seems like a logical place to cut."

"You have got to be kidding. Do you have any idea how much the people here sacrifice and bend over backward to do their jobs? I don't know if you realize how everyone has been pitching in while we backfill Brenda's and the other open positions. Now you're saying we can't even give the staff a proper thank you?"

"You're a creative and resourceful person. Make it work." Grant's cell phone vibrated, interrupting their conversation. He waved his hand dismissively. "I've got to take this. Have a good weekend, Ilsa."

Ilsa walked out of Grant's office with her back straight and her temper ready to boil over. What was she going to do now? She couldn't cancel the event, and with the little money she had to work with she didn't know how she would be able to pull it off. With only three weeks to come up with a celebration that would even remotely be worthy of the hardworking staff of the center, there was a lot to do. If she couldn't come up with something, she feared this might be the final straw for some of the staff members.

Over and over Ilsa had tried to figure out Grant's end game, but she couldn't. Maybe he didn't have one. Maybe he was simply a miserable person and an A-1 jerk with a side of idiot. It didn't matter. Regardless of the reason or reasons, he would not win.

Ilsa sat in her car while it warmed up and tried to get her anger in check. She couldn't let Grant ruin her weekend. She would come up with something. Unfortunately, she had no idea what that something would be. Before she pulled out of the parking lot, she heard her cell phone ding. There was a text message from Dominic.

Meet me at the loft. I'll bring dinner. Clothes are optional.

Marta had gone to visit friends in Cleveland and wouldn't be back until Monday, so they had the place to themselves. She needed to take her mind off her worries, and Dominic was just what the doctor ordered.

Ilsa let herself into Dominic's loft and went straight to the refrigerator. He said he would be bringing dinner home, but she needed a quick snack and knew she could always find something yummy in his refrigerator.

After finishing her snack she still felt tense. Being careful not to fall into the trap of using food to calm her nerves, she purposely walked out of the kitchen. Wandering to another part of the loft, she tried to settle down on the sofa only to end up restlessly flipping through a magazine. Then she remembered she had left a bottle of *Calm* shower gel for Dominic to try. Maybe some aromatherapy and a hot shower would do her some good. Finding what she needed in the bathroom,

Ilsa turned off the lights except for the one in the shower stall, lit a few scented candles, and stepped into what she hoped would be liquid therapy, allowing her stress to melt away.

When Dominic pulled into the parking lot, he immediately noticed Ilsa's car parked in his extra spot. Knowing she was inside waiting for him made him even more anxious to see her. He had been thinking about spending time with her all day, and now that time had finally arrived.

Making his way to the third-floor loft, he walked inside and saw Ilsa's coat and purse, but he didn't see her. A part of him had hoped she would have greeted him at the door wearing nothing but a smile. After calling for her and walking around the loft, he heard the shower running. Even better, he thought.

The combination of hot water cascading over her body, the soft flickering glow of the candlelight, and the soothing scent of ginger, lavender, and other subtle fragrances that filled the room and her senses was enough to bring about a degree of much-needed calm to Ilsa's day. She began to feel better and a lot less angry.

At home, she never took this much time in the shower. Her morning routine didn't allow it. More to the point, there was always a meeting to get to or traffic to consider. However, tonight she indulged. One of the amenities she enjoyed in Dominic's custom-designed bathroom was the oversized showerhead that practically bathed her entire body in its spray. She also loved the spacious vanity, perfect for putting on makeup or when doing her hair.

Realizing how long she had been in the shower, Ilsa decided it was time to get out, especially since her fingers had started to wrinkle. Stepping out of the shower, she was completely oblivious to Dominic as he leaned against the vanity. It wasn't until she reached for a towel that she noticed him.

He heard her gasp and instantly regretted not making his presence known sooner.

"I'm so sorry," he said, quickly apologizing.

Naked and dripping wet, Ilsa went from being frightened to relieved in a matter of seconds. "Dom, you scared me to death! Why didn't you say something? How long have you been standing there?"

Walking over and wrapping her in a towel, he apologized again. "I'm sorry. I didn't mean to frighten you. I came home and didn't see you. Then I heard the water running and saw you enjoying the shower. I didn't want to disturb your peace. I would have joined you, but it seemed like you needed some *me* time."

Ilsa secured the towel around her body and pretended to glare at Dominic.

"Am I forgiven?"

"For what? Scaring me to death or not joining me in the shower?"

Smiling, he replied, "Both, but the second thing more."

Ilsa moved in close to Dominic. Taking his face in her hands, she kissed him passionately. She needed to feel the comfort of his arms around her, the strength of his body pressed to hers, and the warmth of his kiss.

Recognizing the unspoken need, he wrapped his arms around her damp body, deepening the kiss.

"You smell so good," he said when the kiss ended.

"That's because I am good," she replied as the towel came loose and dropped to the floor.

"You know how I love a confident woman," he said, then scooped her up and carried her to his bedroom.

CHAPTER TWENTY-EIGHT

Ilsa woke up in the middle of the night to howling winds and freezing rain pelting the windows. Slipping Dominic's robe over her naked body, she quietly headed to the kitchen.

Looking for something sweet, she hit pay dirt with the leftover chocolate cake Dom had brought home from the restaurant. Pouring herself a glass of milk to go with the cake, she sat on one of the barstools enjoying her snack. Thoughts of the staff appreciation day surfaced again, and she picked up a scratchpad and pen to jot down some ideas.

Hearing footsteps behind her, she turned and saw Dominic approaching with his hair tousled and chest bare. He wore a pair of pajama pants that provided just enough cover to be sexy and functional. He looked even more delicious than the chocolate cake.

"Can't sleep?"

"I was thirsty. Then I saw the chocolate cake and realized I was hungry too. Plus, whatever is going on outside sounds serious."

Dominic went to the refrigerator, looked around inside, and then closed it without taking anything out. Joining Ilsa, he sat down and took a bite of her cake.

"What's that?" he asked, nodding toward the scratchpad.

Ilsa took a deep breath and exhaled slowly. "How much do you love me?" she asked.

"More than chocolate cake and sleeping in on Saturdays. Why?"

"If I kill Grant, would you help me get rid of the body?" she asked jokingly.

"What's he done now?"

"He cut the budget for our staff appreciation day down to the bone. There's barely enough money left for me to do anything worthwhile. Since I don't want to cancel it, I'm trying to come up with a way to do something nice for everyone while at the same time letting them know how much I value everything they do."

"What have you come up with?" Dominic took another bite of cake.

"A pretty sad excuse for an event that nobody will want to attend."

"What's your budget?"

When Ilsa told him, he ran his hand through his hair and shook his head. "It sounds to me like Grant is trying to sabotage the event."

"My thoughts exactly, but I have no idea why except to think that he's been sent here by some unknown enemy of mine to drive me crazy."

Dominic finished the last bite of cake and placed the plate in the sink. "I have an idea."

Giving up, Ilsa placed the pen and paper on the counter. "Please share. At this point, I'm open to anything."

"Let's have it here."

"Here, like at your home?"

Dominic nodded. "I can work with Lu and Milo to come up with a menu. Then you come up with whatever activities you think everyone would like. There's more than enough room here. All we need to do is to get some extra tables and chairs if we need them."

Ilsa smiled sadly and shook her head. "That sounds nice, Dom, but we can't afford you. You know what little I have to work with."

"I know, but I can work with that."

She looked at Dominic skeptically.

"Let me do this for you."

"Why?"

"Because that's what you do when you love someone, and it's less incriminating than burying bodies. Now, stop asking questions, accept my offer, and let's do this."

Ilsa thought about Dominic's offer. She liked the idea, and she knew she couldn't do any better. She began to get excited, and her head spun with ideas about how to make this a truly remarkable event for her staff. "Okay," she said once the idea sunk in. "Let's do this."

"Now," Dominic said, turning off the light in the kitchen. Grabbing Ilsa's hand he headed back to the bedroom. "There's something else you do when you love someone."

Ilsa giggled. "Well, you ate all of my cake. What else do you want?"

"Come back to bed, and I'll show you."

Dominic's cell phone woke them early the next morning. It was Lu calling to see if he had looked out the window at the wintry weather that had blanketed the city overnight. According to Lu, the roads were in horrible condition, and a weather advisory had been issued. This, Dominic knew, would translate into a lot of cancellations and slow business. Lu told him she could handle things at the restaurant, and there was no reason for him to come in until later that afternoon.

"Is everything okay?"

Dominic rolled over, pulling Ilsa close to him. "Lu wanted to let me know that I don't need to come in until later. The roads are in bad shape, and everything is ice-covered."

"Sounds like a good excuse to stay in bed."

"Do we need an excuse?"

Ilsa lay with her head on Dominic's chest, her legs intertwined in his, with the only sound coming from the howling winter wind. She could feel him playing in her hair, something he did so often she didn't even mind anymore.

"I want to ask you something," she said.

"Bacon, eggs, toast, with a side of hash browns."

"I'm serious."

"So am I. I love your hash browns, and you wore me out last night. I'm weak and I need food, woman."

Ilsa smiled and snuggled in closer. They had made love off and on throughout the night as the winter winds howled. Not particularly crazy about winter, she did find the backdrop of wintry sounds, pelting rain, and then seeing the snow falling more than a little romantic.

"Are you complaining that I kept you up all night?"

"That is not what I said!"

"What can I say? You have that effect on me. I guess you could say that I love loving you," she said.

Dominic kissed her on the forehead and stroked her bare arm. And he loved the way she loved him. Discovering each other's likes and dislikes, coupled with the powerful desire to please and satisfy the other, had served to greatly intensify their lovemaking. For him, it was exciting to learn what pleased and excited Ilsa—the sensitive spot at the base of her throat or kissing her on the back of the neck. Even cooking together, an activity they both enjoyed, often turned into sexy play. Ultimately, Dominic strived to leave her satisfied and knowing, without a doubt, that she was loved, wanted, and that he found her to be incredibly sexy.

For Ilsa, being sexually adventurous had taken a little effort, even though Dominic made it easier. She delighted in exploring what turned him on. Learning that he loved to kiss and be kissed allowed her to use that to her advantage. If she wanted to initiate lovemaking, she simply started with a passionate kiss, often licking or tugging on his lower lip. She also knew how much he loved it when she wore sexy underwear. Since that part of her wardrobe had been lacking, she splurged on a few things she thought he might like and that made her feel sexy.

Just recently, on a whim, she had purchased a cream-colored lacy bra and panty set accented with little black bows. She'd almost forgotten that she was wearing them until later that evening. Dominic undressed her, saw the set, and practically drooled. Now, whenever she knew she would be seeing him, she made sure to wear something sexy.

One of the things she liked most was when she and Dominic were in the kitchen together. Most of the time they would start with good intentions, washing or chopping vegetables or preparing the entrée. Dominic would pass to get something from the pantry or refrigerator, and he would kiss her. Often he would have her taste something, or she would feed him a little of what she was making. Fingers would be licked, kisses exchanged, and, before either of them knew it, they were making love in the kitchen.

At the moment, Dominic's fingers were traveling over her curves, sending tingles coursing through her body. She needed to ask him her question before they were both caught up and unable to focus on anything but each other.

"How do you feel about going with me to my father's birthday party?"

"How do *you* feel about me going?"

"Don't answer a question with a question. I want to know if you'll go with me."

Dominic stopped his finger play on Ilsa's body and leaned back so she could see his face. "Why wouldn't I?"

"It might be overwhelming," she warned. "My entire family will be there. Parents, sisters, cousins, aunts and uncles, former neighbors, and even my sons. That's a lot of people to meet all at once."

"I'll be fine," he assured her. "You're a part of my life, and I'm a part of yours. We're in this together. I'm more than willing to meet your family, and I'm looking forward to it."

Pleased that Dominic was excited about meeting her family, Ilsa made a mental note to call her sons and tell them about him before her father's party. She wanted to make sure the only surprise that night was all about her father.

CHAPTER TWENTY-NINE

The wintry weekend weather carried over into the beginning of the week with more snow, ice, blistering winds, and frigid temperatures. Since Cleveland received more snow and ice than Columbus, Marta's return to Columbus had been delayed.

The day before Marta was to leave for Arizona, she and Ilsa had lunch together—just the two of them, without Dominic, at Marta's suggestion.

While she waited for Ilsa to join her at the restaurant, Marta looked out the window. It had stopped snowing, but the wind was still bitter and biting. This was the part about living in Ohio that she didn't miss one bit. It would be nice to be back in the sunshine and warmth.

Ilsa arrived at the restaurant cold and windblown. Looking around for Marta, she saw her sitting at a table near the window. Marta waved her over.

"I'm sorry I'm late."

Marta smiled and shook her head. "You're fine. I've kept myself entertained by people watching. I can't believe how many couples dine together but hardly look up from their phones to speak to each other."

Ilsa looked around the busy restaurant. There was a sizable crowd considering the latest artic intrusion from Old Man Winter. As Marta observed, most of the couples seemed to be paying more attention to their phones than to the person sitting right in front of them. She hoped she never became that complacent with those she cared about, especially with Dominic.

"Are you ready to go back home? I can imagine you've missed your friends and your life in Arizona."

Marta took a sip of hot tea, hoping it would warm her up a bit. "I miss being at home but I miss the sunshine most of all. Oh, yes, and temperatures above seventy degrees," she joked. "It'll be good to get back to my church and volunteering. The work we do with expectant mothers is something I enjoy very much, so if anything, that is what I miss the most. Oh, and sleeping in my bed."

"Well, your son is going to miss you and so am I."

"Thank you, Ilsa. I have enjoyed meeting you, and I think you are a wonderful young woman. Dom is lucky to have you in his life."

The waitress appeared at their table to take their orders. Once she left, Marta turned her attention back to Ilsa. "I've never seen my son so happy. You have brought some things into his life that I don't think he even knew were missing. Joy. Passion. Love."

A little caught off guard by Marta's declaration, Ilsa didn't quite know what to say.

"If you don't mind me asking, have you figured things out yet?"

Ilsa looked puzzled.

"For a while there, you were struggling with your feelings."

Ilsa lowered her eyes and nodded. "I have. The process took some unnecessary turns, and I may have made it more difficult than it should have been, but it worked out."

"I'm glad to hear that," Marta said with a wink. "I believe the last time we spoke about this, you were doing more thinking and less listening to your heart."

Ilsa smiled shyly. "Guilty."

"Will you allow me to give you one more piece of advice?"

Ilsa nodded enthusiastically. Even if she wanted to, could she say no?

"Take care of Dom, and allow him to take care of you. I don't know what plans the two of you have for the future, but whatever they are, always remember how much you love and care for each other. Everything else will take care of itself."

When it was time for Marta to leave, Ilsa went with Dominic to take his mother to the airport. Waiting until Marta disappeared into the crowd after going through the security checkpoint, they walked quietly back to the parking garage. Ilsa hadn't expected to feel emotional as she said her goodbyes to Marta, but she was a little sad to see her go.

That night Ilsa wanted to spend time with Dominic, but she had brought work home that needed to be finished. After Dominic dropped her off at home, she sat on her sofa reading through résumés received for open positions at the center. Unfortunately, she wasn't making much progress and was having a hard time focusing.

Thinking about Marta and the way she talked about her work with the women at her church was something she couldn't stop thinking about. The way her eyes lit up and how excited and passionate she sounded made Ilsa pause. Remembering when she used to experience those same feelings, she now struggled to recall the last time she felt that way.

As she looked over the qualifications of the various applicants, she had to wonder if they would do well and fit in with the rest of the staff at New Hope. Would they go over and above for the women and families they served? She wondered how they would see the women. Would they view them as someone who could be their sister, friend, or mother? What was the likelihood of one of these faceless applicants being someone who made a difference in the life of a woman and wants to continue that feeling by helping even more women? Or would they become like her? Tired. Defeated. Discouraged.

Ilsa placed the stack of résumés aside and stretched out on the sofa. As she took a break she began to think about how much her life had changed in the past year and how much of that change could be affecting her current way of looking at things.

Just recently Dominic had asked her if she thought about a career change. Until now, she had not. What else would she do? Working at New Hope had been such a big part of her life for so long that she couldn't even see herself in another field. She certainly couldn't imagine being back in the corporate world with the politics, bureaucracy, and single-minded focus on the bottom line.

She wondered, was this her mid-life crisis?

Picking up the stack of résumés, she put that thought aside for now. But sooner or later she knew she would have to give it more serious thought before her mid-life crisis turned into a full-on crisis.

CHAPTER THIRTY

Living in the Midwest all her life, Ilsa knew that November weather could mean snow, sleet, and misery. It could also mean unseasonably mild temperatures and abundant sunshine. Unfortunately for her, the forecast called for snow and ice, and Mother Nature delivered. Just one day before the staff appreciation party, the weather appeared to be mocking her as freezing rain pelted her face each time she stepped out of the car.

Looking over her list, she only needed to go to one more store to pick up supplies for the party. Thanks to Dominic, Lu, and Milo, the food would be something she didn't have to worry about. Dominic had arranged for extra tables and chairs to be delivered so everyone would have plenty of room to sit, eat, and socialize.

As she ran her errands, Ilsa made a mental note to do something special for Lu, who, in her opinion, had to be the most amazing person currently in her life, excluding

Dominic. When Ilsa met with her to discuss the menu, Lu had given her several suggestions that were beyond her expectations. Ultimately, they decided on a menu that would be sure to please everyone: stuffed grape leaves with meat and without for the vegetarians, falafel, lamb, chicken, and beef kabobs with rice, hummus, pita, and veggies. But the one thing Ilsa knew her staff would love, and something Lu had suggested, was a sundae bar, complete with three kinds of ice cream, fresh whipped cream, cherries, and a variety of toppings. Lu had also loaned one of the waiters from the restaurant to assist with serving the food.

The only thing lacking at this point was nicer weather.

As she navigated past drivers who seemed to have forgotten how to drive in inclement weather, her cell phone rang.

"Hi. How's my married son?"

"Hey, Mom. I'm doing okay."

"I got your message about Patrice's promotion. I've been very busy, but I'll call later and congratulate her."

"Yeah, she's so excited. I've got some good news too."

Baby news?

"Remember the account I told you we were trying to get?"

"With the company in Barcelona?"

"Yes. Well, we got it. And here's the good news; I've been tapped to lead the account."

Excited for her son, Ilsa congratulated him. She was proud of both her sons. They had chosen careers where they could excel and build successful careers. All of their hard work and her encouraging them to study was finally paying off.

"That was the good news. I have bad news too." Byron continued, "I'm going to be leaving for Barcelona the Monday before Granddad's birthday party. I'll be gone for twelve weeks."

"Oh, no. You're going to miss the party." Ilsa knew her father would be disappointed that his grandson wouldn't be there for the celebration, but he would also be very proud of him once he heard why. Knowing her son, he would make up for his absence with a unique and personalized gift that he would probably deliver himself once he returned.

"Your grandfather will understand," she said. "Just make sure you take the time to call him on his actual birthday. He'll appreciate that."

Byron assured his mother that he would.

"So, Mom, what else has been going on with you? Aunt Imani told me you met someone."

Imani again.

"Well, yes, that's true. I was going to tell you and your brother about that myself. However, it seems Aunt Imani beat me to it. She's quite the teller of family news these days." She tried to keep the sarcasm out of her voice.

"Is he anyone I know?"

Ilsa told her son about Dominic, how they met, and that she had planned to introduce him at the birthday party.

"Now I'm extra sorry that I won't be there. I'd like to size this dude up for myself," Byron said with a chuckle.

Ilsa smiled. Byron had always been her protector and her biggest champion.

"You sound happy."

She thought for a brief moment, then responded, "Yes, Byron, I am."

"Good. I know I never said anything before, but I know you made a lot of sacrifices for us after Dad died. That couldn't have been easy. We were a handful. But all of that is over now. It's your turn to do something for you. You deserve it."

Ilsa ended the call with her son just as she pulled into her driveway. She sat for a minute before getting out. Her boys had turned out okay after all. Actually, better than okay.

There were many times after her husband died that she worried if she was enough for them. Could she be everything they needed? Just as Byron had said, they were indeed a handful. Eventually, raising the boys got a little easier. She stopped worrying and did the best she could. In the end, and with a lot of love, chaos, hugs, and conversations, her boys had turned into good men.

CHAPTER THIRTY-ONE

Ilsa had been trying to get in touch with Tia for over a week. She had gotten a call from her program director letting Ilsa know that she had missed several classes. Because the program was accelerated, if she missed any more without making them up, she wouldn't be allowed to complete the program.

She had scheduled an appointment with Tia for two o'clock that afternoon. While she waited for her to show up, or not show up as was her habit, Ilsa did her best to avoid Grant, who seemed to be in quite a nasty mood.

"Hey, do you have a second?"

Ilsa looked up from her work and motioned Priscilla into her office.

"Sure. What's up?"

Stepping inside, Priscilla closed the door, taking a seat across from her boss. "I just want to say how much I enjoyed the employee appreciation day. You did a wonderful job with the food and activities. Usually, everyone eats, hangs out for a little while to be polite, and then leaves. Not this time. Everyone wanted to hang around, talk, and participate in the activities. The whole office is still talking about it."

Ilsa was pleased. If it weren't for Dominic and Lu, she didn't know what she would have been able to pull together.

"I'm glad everyone had a good time."

"How did you get Dominic's restaurant to cater?"

"That's a long story. Did you like the food?"

"No, I loved the food! I was telling my husband about it, and he made reservations for the two of us last week. The food was just as good. We'll definitely be going back. Maybe we'll run into Dominic the next time we're there."

"Hey, change of subject; did you distribute the latest applications for intake?"

"Yes, I did that this morning. We've already set up the initial appointments."

"Great. You're a lifesaver. If I haven't told you lately, I appreciate everything you do around here. I don't feel as if I say that enough."

Priscilla stood to leave. "And we appreciate you. Don't think the staff hasn't noticed everything you do around here, including keeping Grant off our asses."

Smiling as Priscilla exited, her smile quickly faded when Grant walked in. He didn't even ask if she was busy when he took a seat across from her.

"Yes, Grant. How can I help you?" she asked, never looking up from her computer.

"I wanted to go over some talking points for the community meeting tomorrow."

Ilsa stopped what she was doing and looked up. "What talking points? We are there to share information about New Hope, hand out brochures, and take questions."

"So you don't have talking points?"

"I have a slide presentation, but it's no different than the countless other presentations I've given."

"I'd like to see it."

Ilsa could feel her face getting hot, but she refused to allow him to throw her off her game. "Grant, what is this really about? Are you planning to attend the meeting?"

"Yes, I am, and I will be making the presentation. A lot is going on here, and I think it would be the best use of your time to be here at the office. This will also be a good opportunity for me to get out into the community as the face of New Hope."

"You?" She struggled to think of what to say next.

"Yes," he said, as he stood to leave. "Please send the presentation before the end of the day today."

Ilsa sat at her desk staring blankly at her computer monitor. *What just happened?* She along with a staff member from New Hope had made these presentations countless times. It usually involved them explaining the services they offered, sharing some of the success stories, and leaving information to distribute to women the partner organizations came into contact with that might need their services. Now Grant felt this wasn't a good use of her time as if he knew how she spent her time. He had no idea!

As she quietly fumed, she didn't even notice Tia standing in her doorway waiting to come in.

"Miss Tanner?"

Ilsa looked up and stared blankly at Tia. It took her a few seconds to remember that they had an appointment.

She waved her inside.

"Is everything okay?" Tia asked.

Ilsa forced a smile and tried to push the conversation she just had with Grant to the back of her mind. "Yes, everything is fine. How are you, Tia? I've been trying to reach you."

"Yes, I know," Tia replied, fidgeting with the zipper on her coat.

"Are you still working?"

Tia nodded.

"Is everything okay at home?"

More fidgeting.

She was distracted, and Ilsa could tell she had something on her mind.

"Tia, remember, we are here to help you. I found out that you've missed some of your classes. I know there are make-up sessions on Saturdays, but you can't miss too many more classes or you'll have to drop out of the program."

She nodded. "I know and I'm sorry I missed the classes. I like learning how to code. It's not something I thought I would ever do, but it's kind of fun."

"So, what happened? What's going on?"

Tia sighed. "It's my boyfriend. He called me last month and wanted to get back together."

Ilsa knew where this was going, but she continued to hear her out.

"He has a good job now, and he asked me to move back in."

"Did you?"

She nodded.

"We're trying to make this work. I even picked up some extra shifts at work to help with the bills and so we can get a car. Plus, with the holidays coming up, the extra money will help with that too. That's why I missed class."

Ilsa knew from Tia's counselor that she was doing very well in class. She also knew Tia felt that she had no one in her corner except the boyfriend. That was his hold over her.

Tia had stopped fidgeting but was uncomfortable. Ilsa wanted so badly to tell her that the boyfriend wasn't someone who was looking out for her best interest; otherwise, he would not have kicked her out the first time and left her to fend for herself. If he truly cared about her he would be encouraging her to better herself instead of working herself to death at a dead-end job.

Ilsa knew she had to tread lightly or risk alienating Tia, so she kept her thoughts about the boyfriend to herself. She also knew from experience that no matter the situation, a person had to see for themselves the consequences of their decisions. In this case, Tia would have to see the boyfriend's true colors for herself and act accordingly.

"Tia, I want you to do what's best for you. It's not selfish to think about your future, and it's not selfish to try to make your life better. It's great that you want to try to make things work with your boyfriend, but keep in mind you still have to look out for yourself. You're smart, ambitious, and you're a survivor. You have the power over your life right now. It's up to you how you use that power."

CHAPTER THIRTY-TWO

Ilsa and Dominic dropped their luggage off at the hotel and headed over to help her sisters. They were to meet Ilsa's sisters, their husbands, and a few other friends to decorate for the surprise birthday party.

This time it was Dominic's turn to be nervous. Later that evening he would be meeting Ilsa's family for the first time. All of them. Now he truly understood how she felt meeting his mother, except in this situation, there were many more people to impress.

Ilsa hadn't said much since they left Columbus and now, even though he knew she was happy about spending time with her family over the weekend, she remained quiet.

On the drive over, Dominic asked, "Your family knows I'm here with you, right?"

When he didn't get an answer, he looked over and noticed her staring blankly ahead, appearing to be a million miles away.

"Ilsa?"

"I'm sorry. Did you say something?"

He reached over and took hold of her hand. "Hey, where are you right now?"

Ilsa had told Dominic about her latest run-in with Grant. She was still angry, not because Grant had pulled a "let me take the lead on this" move, but because she repeatedly allowed him to get under her skin.

She had also shared a little about Tia, without mentioning her name and the exact situation, but enough to let Dominic know that she was concerned that one of her clients was letting a great opportunity slip through her fingers because of a boyfriend that Ilsa was pretty sure was using her and would be kicking her out again.

And the final blow came when Ilsa's eldest son called to say he had the flu and wouldn't be able to make the party. She was truly disappointed about not seeing either of her sons and being able to introduce them to Dominic.

Dominic hated seeing her like this, distracted, tense, and so lost in her thoughts that she tuned everything and everyone out. He knew how much her job meant to her and how much she cared. But he could also see how much it was stressing her out lately.

He was losing count of the number of times she bought work home, stayed late at the office, or went in on the weekend. All of that coupled with worrying about who from New Hope would be the next to quit was causing Ilsa to change. Dominic saw it. He wondered if she did too.

"Listen, I know this is easier said than done, but do me a favor and try not to let everything that's going on at work ruin your weekend. There's absolutely nothing you can do about it right now anyway. After this weekend, we'll put our heads together and come up with a strategy to deal with New Hope. Right now, focus on your family, your dad's party, and enjoying this time with the people who care about you. How does that sound?"

Dominic was right. She would not allow her work worries to seep into the little free time that she had nor take away from the joy of spending time with the people she loved. For now, she would tuck it all away and deal with it later.

"You're right, and I think it sounds like a good plan," she said, doing her best to smile and mean it.

When they arrived at the community center where the party would be taking place, the preparations were in full swing. Streamers and banners were being hung, and a small team was in charge of blowing up and bundling balloons. In the center of it all, Ilsa spotted her big sister, organizing and delegating as only she could.

Ilsa took Dominic's hand and led him in that direction. When Ivy saw her sister approaching, she stopped mid-sentence with her instructions as a big smile spread across her face.

After the two sisters exchanged hugs, Ivy gave her sister a look, turned to Dominic, and then back to her sister.

"And this is Dominic," Ivy remarked.

"Dominic, this is my *oldest* sister, Ivy."

Ivy playfully cut her eyes at her sister and extended her hand to Dominic.

After exchanging pleasantries, Ivy assigned Dominic the task of placing tablecloths on the tables, then she whisked Ilsa away.

In a private corner of the room, Ivy looked around to make sure no one could overhear their conversation.

"Did you forget to mention one small detail about Dominic?"

Knowing exactly what her sister meant, Ilsa downplayed the question. "What...that he's tall, dark, and handsome?"

Ivy pursed her lips. "Seriously, Ilsa?"

"Oh, you mean the other thing," she remarked sarcastically.

"Look, you know I don't care who you date, but this is something you might have thought to mention all the times we've talked."

Ilsa sat down at an empty table. "Do these need to be folded?" she asked, nodding toward the stack of programs for the party.

"Yes," Ivy replied and sat across from her.

"I didn't mention that Dominic wasn't Black because I didn't think it would or should be a big deal."

"I agree. But not mentioning it kind of made it one."

"Do you think anyone else will care?"

"Well, considering it's no longer 1955, this conversation really shouldn't be a conversation at all, but people are people, Ilsa. Some people are going to have a problem with you and Dominic being together, and some won't give it a second thought. You know I'm the latter group. But for anyone who gives you a hard time, send them my way and I'll be more than happy to set them straight."

Dominic worked steadily, placing the tablecloths on each table as he had been instructed. Per Ivy's direction, each one must be hung uniformly. To be exact, the second seam had to be square with the edge of the table.

As he worked, he occasionally stole glances in the direction of Ilsa and her sister as they continued talking. Judging by the bowed heads and the look on Ilsa's face, he wondered if he was the topic of discussion or, more specifically, his and Ilsa's relationship. He hoped there wouldn't be any issues.

"Don't worry about those two."

Dominic turned toward the voice.

"Hi. I'm Malik, Ivy's husband."

The two men shook hands.

"You look worried."

"Looks like a pretty serious conversation is going on over there."

Malik shrugged and began helping Dominic with the tablecloths.

"I'm sure it's nothing serious. A case of the big sister looking out for her younger sister. You should have seen the huddle Ivy had with her sisters when they first met me!"

Dominic tried to figure out the tone of the conversation by Ilsa's body language and facial expressions, but he had no idea what they were talking about as they sat folding programs.

Malik continued to engage Dominic in conversation while they worked. It was the least he could do. The poor guy had actually broken out in a sweat!

"Ivy tells me you own a pretty nice restaurant in Columbus."

"Yes, YiaYia's Table."

"I make it to Columbus a few times out of the year for training and meetings."

"You're a police officer, right?"

"Detective," Malik remarked proudly. "I serve in the same unit as Imani's husband."

Imani. Another sister he had yet to meet. *What would that reception be like*, Dominic wondered.

"Look," Malik said, hoping to put Dominic at ease. "You're going to be meeting a lot of family members tonight. You need to relax. Don't let that little huddle over there worry you. Ilsa and her sisters are very close. They may disagree with each other, and they sometimes get mad when one of them does something the others don't like, but at the end of the day they are sisters to the core. They support and respect each other no matter what. I'm sure Ivy is just giving Ilsa the third degree to make sure everything is good and she's happy."

Although he'd only just met Malik, Dominic liked him. His pep talk was beginning to have an effect.

"Judging by the way Ilsa talks about you to Ivy and Imani, you make her *very* happy. And it's hard on a brother too! For weeks I had to hear about that picnic you took Ilsa on."

The two men shared a laugh.

"No time for idle chitchat," Ivy warned when she walked up on her husband and Dominic.

Malik turned to Dominic with a knowing look. "When the boss lady speaks, I listen."

"Dominic, can you go over and help Ilsa? Malik and I will finish the tables."

He looked at Malik who gave him a "don't question the order, just follow it" look. He complied.

"Did your sister give you a hard time about me?" he asked when he joined Ilsa at the table.

"No. But she did ask why I didn't tell her you were smoking hot."

Dominic smiled at Ilsa's attempt at a joke, but he needed to make sure everything was all right.

"Seriously, Ilsa."

Ilsa took a break from folding programs and smiled reassuringly.

"Everything is perfectly fine. Relax. Ivy is happy that I'm happy."

And with that, Dominic dropped the subject, relaxed, and picked up a stack of programs.

"He's what?" Imani asked as she strained to hear her sister over the noise of the bakery.

"Greek and Italian," Ivy repeated. "I wanted to tell you before you showed up tonight."

"What's Italian?"

"Oh, good lord, Imani. Can you find someplace quiet for a second?"

Imani grabbed a number. While she waited to be served, she stepped into a corner of the busy bakery where she could focus on the conversation with her sister.

"Okay. Say what you said again."

"Ilsa's new man, he's not Black. He's White. She said he's Italian and Greek. I wanted to tell you before you showed up tonight at the party," she repeated with a little more detail this time.

"Is he fine?" she asked with Imani-like indifference.

"Yes, he certainly is that."

"Do Mom and Dad know?"

"I doubt it."

"Do you think they'll care?"

"They never did with any of the guys you used to bring home, so why would they care with Ilsa?"

"Hey, they just called my number. If we want rolls and a cake for tonight, I've got to run. This isn't a big deal, Ivy. Please don't make it one."

CHAPTER THIRTY-THREE

"Surprise!" the entire room shouted in unison when Virgil Dixon stepped into the room.

Amidst a chorus of "happy birthday" and "congratulations, old man," he was truly surprised and overwhelmed by the celebration, but was most pleased to be surrounded by his closest friends and family.

When the opportunity presented itself, Ilsa found her father and pulled him away from the festivities for a few minutes. He wrapped her in a bear hug, the same way he used to when she was a little girl. She missed those hugs.

"Happy birthday, Daddy," Ilsa said as she quickly brushed away a tear.

"Why are you crying, sweetheart?" Virgil asked.

Ilsa hadn't meant to get sentimental, but being home around her family and seeing how much her father was enjoying himself gave her such a wonderful feeling. Not one to take things for granted, she also recognized how blessed she was to still have both her parents in her life.

"It's just good to be home and seeing everyone, that's all."

Vigil folded his middle daughter in his arms and gave her another hug. While he loved all of his daughters, Ilsa held a special place in his heart and had ever since she was a little girl. His wife always said Ilsa was the most like him in temperament, attitude, and spirit. He thought so too.

"I can't believe you girls did all of this," he exclaimed excitedly as he took in the decorations, food, and people who filled the room.

"We wanted to do something special. It's not every day you turn eighty."

"Well, this certainly is special."

Ruby, who seemed just as thrilled with how everything came together, joined her husband and daughter the same time Dominic walked up. He had been standing nearby talking to Malik when Ilsa beckoned him.

Time to meet the parents.

"Mom, Dad, I want you to meet someone special. This is Dominic Markos."

Dominic started to put his arm around Ilsa's waist then thought better of it. Resting his hand on her shoulder or even holding her hand didn't seem right either. He immediately felt like a kid meeting his girlfriend's shotgun-wielding father and desperately wanting to make a good impression.

"Happy birthday, sir," he said, extending his hand to Virgil.

Despite his age, Virgil's grip was strong and his gaze steady. "I've heard a lot about you."

No smile. No frown either. Dominic couldn't tell anything from Virgil's expression or the intense eye contact he seemed determined to maintain.

Ruby interceded when she noticed the small beads of perspiration dotting Dominic's brow.

"It's nice to meet you, Dominic. Ilsa told us all about your restaurant and your skills in the kitchen. It just so happens that I looked up your restaurant online, and I see you've gotten some wonderful reviews. And the menu looks amazing. Virgil and I will have to visit the next time we're in town."

"You...you looked up his restaurant *online?*" Ilsa asked her seventy-eight-year-old mother, who only three years earlier had gotten her first smartphone.

"Yes, sweetheart, I'm quite the web surfer these days. Not too long ago the church offered a basic computer class for older adults, and I took it. The instructor said I'm a natural. Turns out there's very little one can't find on the internet, especially if you have the time to do the research," she replied as she linked arms with her husband and turned to walk away.

Dominic met the amused look on Ilsa's face with a puzzled one of his own.

"That," she remarked with a wry smile, "was my mother's way of letting me know that she knew who you were even before I introduced you. She's done her research."

"Research?"

"I won't say she cyber-stalked you, but..."

Dominic was having a good time. The slide show tribute Virgil's daughters put together had everyone laughing and even shedding a few tears. The remarks given by family and friends were a testament to a man who was well-loved and respected.

Throughout the evening Dominic quietly observed Ilsa's interactions with her family and friends. He paid special attention to the exchanges between her and her sisters. He already knew they spoke often on the phone, but he now had a first-hand view of just how close the sisters were.

Having already met Ivy, Dominic mentally prepared to properly meet Ilsa's youngest sister, who Malik had described as the quintessential baby sister. Imani had breezed in right before the party began, greeted her sisters, and briefly introduced herself to him. However, she did warn him that they would need to talk more before the weekend was over.

Not quite sure what she had in mind, Dominic could only wait and hope for the best.

"Ilsa Tanner. Girl, you look as good as ever."

Ilsa turned from the conversation she was having with her parents' neighbor and stood face-to-face with Omar Goodwin, former big deal in high school, ex-husband to three wives, and current insurance sales agent. Omar had been someone Ilsa had gone out with a grand total of two times after her husband died.

Politely excusing herself from her current conversation, she smiled at Omar and at the same time wondered who had invited him to her father's party, and why.

Omar could very well be considered one of the most self-centered and boring men she had ever spent time with in her life. For some odd reason, he had wormed his way into her parents' lives and was always around when she came for a visit. It had been her mother's idea that she go out with Omar, an idea she bet had originated with him. At first, she had declined his invitations for dinner, drinks, and whatever. However, she eventually agreed to a date, partially to appease her mother but also because at that time she had been feeling lonely and needed a break from reality. Although, soon after, she realized she had made a big mistake. Omar may have been charming around her parents, but with her he was pushy, arrogant, and made her feel as if she should have been grateful to be out with him. To make matters worse, she gave him a second chance, but his behavior hadn't improved one bit.

Omar grabbed her unexpectedly and awkwardly hugged her.

"Okay, wow," she exclaimed once he released her, but he remained too close for her comfort.

"You look good," he said. "I think you get prettier every time I see you, which has been quite a while."

Ilsa forced a smile. Usually, she did an effective job of avoiding him whenever she came to Cincinnati, but he would occasionally catch her at her parents'.

"How long are you going to be in the city? Maybe we can get together and..."

Instead of finishing his thought, he ran his fingertips down her arm.

Annoyed, Ilsa took a step back. She wasn't attracted to Omar in the least, and it had nothing to do with Dominic. She had no intention of continuing this cat-and-mouse game with him. It was time to put a stop to his pursuits.

"Hey, sweetheart, your sisters wanted me to come and get you for the cake cutting." Dominic came up behind Ilsa, placing his arm around her waist and pulling her to him.

Caught off guard and surprised, Omar looked from Ilsa to Dominic and back to Ilsa. Getting the hint, he mumbled something under his breath and walked away.

If she had a camera she would have recorded the look on Omar's face for posterity. Somehow, she didn't think she would be running into him any time soon. Hopefully, there wouldn't be any more "surprise" visits from him at her parents' house either.

Turning to face Dominic, she asked, "What was that all about?"

With a smug look on his face, Dominic replied, "That was about me noticing the look on your face when that guy stepped up to you and me letting him know you're mine."

After everyone sang "Happy Birthday" and Virgil blew out his candles, Imani, Ivy, and Ilsa made their way around the room serving cake to the guests of the party. When she reached the table where Dominic was sitting, Imani called her husband over and handed her tray off to him. She took the empty seat beside Dominic.

"Are you enjoying the party?"

Dominic nodded. "I am."

"Good. I'm glad we had a chance to finally meet you. My sister likes you. A lot."

Feeling a little uneasy, Dominic replied, "And I like her a lot."

"That's good. I want you to know that I love my sister. She means the world to me. The two of you seem happy together, but if the time comes and you're not, don't hurt her. She has been through a lot. The last thing she needs to deal with is a broken heart."

"I have no intentions of ever hurting Ilsa," he said, meaning every word.

"Good," Imani said as she stood to leave. "See, that wasn't hard at all. Enjoy the rest of the party."

The party wrapped up with everyone making plans to meet the next day. After helping to load the presents into Virgil's car and dividing up the remaining food, they called it a night.

Back at the hotel, Ilsa undressed and fell into bed, physically tired but pleased with how the evening turned out. She had seen family, friends, and neighbors that she hadn't seen in years. And her father had been over the moon with the laughter, food, fun, and fellowship.

"Tired?" Dominic asked as he slipped in bed beside her.

"Exhausted," she said, snuggling next to him. She inhaled. He was wearing the aftershave her lady had mixed just for him, and Ilsa loved it. Manly, but not overpowering. Earthy with just a hint of spice, and uniquely him.

"Your mom asked if we were coming back next week for Thanksgiving."

"She did? She didn't ask me."

"She also said she'd be serving breakfast tomorrow at eight. The way she said it sounded more like an expectation than a suggestion."

"I know. She'll have everything ready at seven forty-five, so no one will have an excuse to skip church. To be honest, I don't know if my body is going to allow me to be fully functional that early in the morning. I'm good with church, but breakfast probably won't be happening for me."

"Just in case you're wondering, I loved tonight."

"Hmm?"

"I mean everything. Your family. Meeting your sisters and their husbands. Your father, who was a little intimidating at first but mellowed quite a bit throughout the night. And the food was amazing; I'm still in awe of that smoked brisket. I even loved meeting and talking to your mother, who cleverly grilled me about stuff that I think she already knew the answers to. All of it." He didn't mention his brief chat with Imani. "It was more fun than I imagined."

"I'm glad," Ilsa responded through a yawn. "They liked you too. Expect them to show up at the restaurant when they come to town."

Something about meeting Ilsa's family made him feel even closer to her. Seeing her with her sisters had given him another glimpse into how she interacted with those she loved. He had even gleaned that she was her father's favorite—not from any overt words or gestures but something unspoken that he had picked up on. His only regret was that he did not meet Ilsa's sons. He would have to make that happen.

Dominic pulled Ilsa closer to him. He loved holding her like this. Hearing her breathe, feeling her smooth skin against his, drinking in her scent—whatever that might be at the moment—and the way her hair fell in whatever direction it wanted. He loved this feeling, and he loved her.

"Ilsa?"

"Yes, baby?" she responded sleepily.

Before he could continue, he was interrupted by his cell phone.

"Hey, Agda. What's up?"

Ilsa felt Dominic's body stiffen. The next words she heard sent a chill straight down her spine.

"What hospital? I'll be on the first flight out."

CHAPTER THIRTY-FOUR

Dominic had reached his maximum caffeine limit hours ago but still grabbed another cup as he exited the airport. On the taxi ride to the hospital, he tried to prepare himself for the worst. Agda had given him very few details over the phone. Their mother had collapsed at the church where she had been volunteering. Upon arriving at the hospital, she was unresponsive but still breathing. He didn't know if she'd had a heart attack or stroke or if it was something else entirely. All he knew was his mother was in the hospital, and he needed to get to her.

Pulling up to the hospital's entrance, Dominic paid the cab fare, grabbed his bag, and steeled himself against whatever news was waiting for him inside.

Exiting the elevator, he saw Agda sitting in the family waiting room directly across the hall. She looked up when she heard the door open.

After exchanging a brief hug with his sister, he quickly registered the worried look on her face. She had been crying, and it looked as if she hadn't slept in days.

"The nurses are changing shifts, so I had to wait out here until someone lets me know when I can go back in," she said.

Dominic couldn't help but notice how weak his sister sounded.

"Where's Nick?"

"He went downstairs to get something to eat."

"Who's watching the kids?"

"Nick's parents."

"Do you know any more about what's going on?"

Agda shook her head. "They're still running tests. MRI. EKG. Cat Scan."

Dominic nodded. Realizing he was still holding the same cup of coffee he'd bought at the airport, he sat down and took a sip. The coffee had gotten cold, but he didn't seem to notice or care. He needed to see his mother. He needed to touch her hand, look into her face, hear her breathing, and know that she was still herself.

Nick walked into the waiting room, completely unnoticed by Dominic or Agda.

"Hey," he said.

Dominic looked up when he felt a hand on his shoulder. Standing to greet his brother-in-law, he felt better knowing he was there for his sister.

"I've got some fruit and a bagel," he said, offering the scant meal to Dominic and Agda.

Agda shook her head, but he coaxed her into eating a couple of bites of bagel.

While they waited for the shift change to be over, Nick engaged Dominic in small talk, trying to do anything he could to ease his worry.

After what seemed like an eternity, someone came out and told them they could go back in to see Marta. Only one visitor was allowed at a time. Agda agreed to let her brother go first.

Once again, Dominic attempted to prepare himself for the unexpected. He needed to be strong.

Near the end of the hall, his steps slowed as he slowly pushed open the door to enter his mother's room. There she was, lying in the hospital bed connected to oxygen, a heart monitor, and other machines that he couldn't readily identify, Dominic paused before entering the room. His heart skipped a beat when he saw how frail she looked as she lay unresponsive and disassociated from everything around her.

Leaning over to kiss her cheek, he pulled up a chair and took a seat at her bedside. Dominic reached out and took his mother's hand in his. It felt so small and lifeless. Since she was unable to hold his hand, he did it for her, wrapping his other hand over hers, covering it completely.

Dominic couldn't ever remember feeling as helpless as he did at that moment. His mind raced with thoughts he couldn't prevent. Trying to redirect his thoughts was an exercise in futility as the reality of what he saw in front of him illustrated how serious the situation was.

He couldn't lose his mother. But he couldn't be selfish either. If it was truly her time to go, he didn't want her to suffer as he held on to a life that no longer belonged to this world.

Bowing his head he admonished himself for thinking that way. He had to be positive. His mother was strong. The doctors didn't even know what was wrong. He needed to hold out hope that they would find the problem and fix it. For now, that was his prayer.

After what seemed like only minutes, Dominic was awakened by someone gently shaking his shoulder and calling his name. Slightly disoriented, he soon recognized his sister as she stood over him holding a cup of coffee.

Unfolding his tall frame and moving his leg over the side of the waiting room couch, he stretched in an attempt to work out the kinks in his back, neck, and shoulders.

"Thanks," he said, taking the cup. "Any news?"

"The doctor is supposed to be here soon. That's why I woke you. The results of the tests should be back, and she should be able to give us some news."

Dominic nodded. "Give me a few minutes to splash some water on my face, and we can wait for her in Mom's room."

In the small bathroom off the family waiting area, Dominic leaned over the sink staring as water circled the stainless steel bowl and ran down the drain. Every movement felt monumental. Willing himself to cup his hands under the stream of water, his arms and legs felt like lead. And his head was filled with so many scattered thoughts he couldn't sort them out.

He wondered what would change after the conversation with his mother's doctor. Would their lives now be measured by before and after? But more troubling, what would after look like?

Agda, Nick, and Dominic spotted Dr. Oyedele, their mother's doctor, standing outside of her room looking at something on a small tablet. She looked up when she heard footsteps.

"Good morning, family," she greeted her patient's children.

As they stepped into Marta's room, Dominic glanced over at his mother who seemed to be sleeping peacefully, oblivious to everything going on around her.

Without wasting time, Dr. Oyedele began to share the results of the tests that had been performed since Marta arrived.

"A heart attack?" Agda questioned. "This was a heart attack?"

Dr. Oyedele nodded and began to explain the results of the EKG and the subsequent treatment that was scheduled for later that morning.

"Is she in a coma?" Dominic asked.

"No. She was given something to help her sleep." Dr. Oyedele typed something into the mobile computer at Marta's bedside. "I also wanted to talk about your mother's medications."

"What about them?" Agda asked, knowing how meticulous her mother was about taking her prescribed medications and herbal supplements.

"Older adults tend to take more medications than younger individuals. While these medications are intended to help treat health issues and manage symptoms, there is also a higher risk of drug interactions. This sometimes causes accidental overdoses."

"She overdosed?"

Dr. Oyedele nodded. "While your mother is here, we'll work with her primary care physician to re-evaluate her medications."

On her way out of the room, Dr. Oyedele assured Marta's family that she was receiving the best care possible. "You'll be able to talk to your mother after her procedure."

Agda and Dominic looked at each other, daring to hope that everything would indeed be okay.

Ilsa sat at her desk looking down at but not actually focusing on a stack of invoices waiting to be approved for payment. Once again she questioned why she had even come in to work. After driving back to Columbus with Dominic so he could pack a bag and catch a flight to Arizona, she had been unable to sleep or get anything done. Her worry for Marta consumed her thoughts. She could only imagine Dominic's state of mind at the hospital as he wondered if his mother would be all right.

Ilsa had never seen Dominic look so worried or afraid. He needed her. He hadn't said it. He didn't need to. She had felt it when she embraced him after he had gotten the news from his sister and heard it in his voice when he said good-bye at the airport.

He hadn't outright asked her if she would come with him, but it was implied. She had declined before he could form the question, saying she wished she could go with him but now wasn't a good time with everything going on at New Hope. Saying those words and leaving him alone during a time she knew he needed her the most broke her heart. Had she broken his as well?

CHAPTER THIRTY-FIVE

"What's she like?"

Dominic turned his attention away from his phone and looked up at his sister. "Huh?"

"Ilsa. Tell me about her."

Nick had gone to get them something to eat while they waited in the family area for their mother's procedure to be over.

"Mom told me a little about her when she got back from her visit with you. She liked her, a lot."

Dominic nodded. "Yeah, they spent quite a bit of time together."

"Mom said she's very smart, very pretty, and a lot of fun," Agda remarked, hoping to coax a little more information out of her brother, who for some reason seemed even more distracted than he was when he first arrived.

"Yeah, she is."

Nick arrived with their food, and he and Agda became caught up in their own conversation, leaving Dominic to his private thoughts.

A member of the cleaning staff came into the waiting area to empty the trash and tidy up a bit. Several nurses stood in the hallway looking over supplies on a cart. An orderly transported a patient in a wheelchair down the hall. It seemed odd to Dominic that everyone and everything seemed to carry on as normal despite the feeling that his whole world had been turned upside down within a matter of days. And he was hanging on by a thread.

Looking down at his phone, he reread the unsent message for Ilsa. The short message offered a synopsis of his mother's diagnosis. He also explained that they would know more about her prognosis after her procedure. He had yet to send the message for one simple reason; those words didn't reflect what was truly on his mind and his heart.

What he really wanted her to know was that he was tired—more tired than he could ever remember being. His body was sore from sleeping on a couch half the length of his body; his mind raced from worry and contemplating too many what-ifs for his own good. He wished that he had the words to tell her that his mother meant the world to him, and so did she. But since there was no way for him to summarize in a series of words just how much his heart ached right now, he sent his original message, wondering if she would be able to read between the lines.

⁓ℓℓ⁓

Ilsa sat at the restaurant waiting for Denita to arrive. She looked over the text message from Dominic where he explained what was going with his mother. The message was short and to the point.

"Hey."

Ilsa looked up from her phone and gave Denita a quick smile.

"From Dominic?" Denita asked, nodding toward Ilsa's phone.

Ilsa nodded.

"How's his mother doing?"

"Better. She had some procedure after her heart attack. Dom said right now she's very weak and has developed an infection on top of everything else."

Denita gave the waitress her order and turned her attention back to Ilsa. "So how is Dominic doing? This has to be pretty rough on him."

"I'm sure it is."

"What's he saying when you two talk?"

"Not much. We've only talked once or twice. Usually, he sends me a text message."

"I see," Denita remarked.

The waitress brought their food, and Ilsa waited for her to leave before replying to Denita. "Go ahead and say it."

"Say what?"

"Tell me that I should be by Dominic's side. Tell me that I was wrong for not going to Arizona to be with him. Tell me that if the situation were reversed, he would move heaven and earth to support me."

"It sounds like I don't need to tell you anything."

Exasperated, Ilsa sat her fork down and pushed her plate away. "Denita, what am I doing? I'm a horrible girlfriend or partner or whatever it is I'm supposed to be in this relationship. I stayed behind because of my job, but when I'm there I'm miserable and I feel pretty useless. I honestly don't even know if I'm making a difference anymore."

Denita raised her eyebrows but continued eating. Knowing Ilsa and how her mind worked, she was going to have to travel down this road of discovery all by herself.

"With everything Dominic has going on in his life right now, the one person he should have been able to count on was me. And what did I do? Absolutely nothing."

Denita sat her fork down, paused for a few seconds, looked at her friend, then said point-blank, "You stayed because you thought the people at New Hope needed you. Right now, you have to ask yourself who needs you more. You know Dominic better than anyone, and you alone know what he needs right now. You're sitting here beating yourself up because you think you've let him down. I'm not saying you did or you didn't. Only you know the answer to that. And only you are in a position to do something about it. The way I see it, you're holding all the cards. What's your next move?"

CHAPTER THIRTY-SIX

It had been a long, restless night, and the workday didn't seem as if it would be any better. It had snowed the previous night, and the drive into work had been slow, messy, and aggravating.

Half the staff was late, and several clients had called in to cancel their appointments. Ilsa was sure some appointments that hadn't already canceled would end up as no shows.

Thanksgiving was a few days away, and she would typically be prepared to either go home to Cincinnati or would be finalizing plans with Denita or her other friends. This year she wouldn't be doing any of that. She wasn't in much of a mood to celebrate anyway.

Ilsa switched on her computer and opened up her email. The first thing she saw was a memo from Grant with the subject line *New Office Processes and Procedures.*

Reluctantly, Ilsa opened the email and began reading. By the time she reached the fifth item on the list, she locked her computer and headed straight to Grant's office. She knew he was in because she had seen his car in the parking lot. It was one of the rare times he was in early. When she got to his office, he was on the phone. Undaunted, she stepped inside and closed the door behind her.

Surprised, Grant looked up and pointed to the phone as if she couldn't see he was talking. She didn't budge.

After completing his call, he started typing something on his computer, not even trying to hide that he was annoyed with Ilsa for barging into his office, something he never thought twice about doing to other people. "What is it?" he snapped. "I've got some calls to return and a few emails I need to get out."

"That's why I'm here, to talk to you about your email."

Grant looked up, puzzled.

"The email you sent to the staff outlining new processes and procedures. What is that all about, Grant? We never talked about this, and I would think this is exactly the kind of thing we would discuss before implementing."

"I am perfectly within my rights to put these changes in place."

"This is bigger than your rights. I don't know if you've been paying attention, but staff morale is at an all-time low. Now, when everyone gets in this morning after dealing with the snow and all the traffic headaches, they will see this list you sent out telling them they can no longer have personal items at their desks and they have to shorten their lunches to thirty minutes. In case you didn't know, most of us already work through lunch because we're so short-staffed. On top of that, you want everyone to pitch in to clean our work areas, restrooms, and break room because you've ended the contract with our janitorial company? What the hell?"

Grant stopped what he was doing long enough to confront Ilsa, who he felt was blatantly overstepping her bounds. "You're questioning my authority?" he asked, red-faced and angry.

Closing her eyes momentarily as she struggled to maintain her composure, she slowly opened them, staring incredulously at Grant. "I am beyond questioning what you do. Obviously, your vision for New Hope is yours and yours alone, and we are here to serve that need. From the moment you came here, you've done nothing but create and fuel a very toxic environment. As a result, I have seen our staff dwindle to almost unmanageable levels. And the brave souls who stayed out of loyalty, love for their job, and because of a genuine desire to serve others, they now feel as if they are expendable. You're either oblivious to the fact that our staff is overworked, discouraged, and just plain tired, or you don't give a damn. Either way, this tone-deaf memo of yours will only make things worse. If I didn't know better, I'd swear you were trying to destroy this agency by getting everyone to quit. If that truly is the case, let me be the first to offer my congratulations. You win."

$\sim\!\!ell\sim$

It was the day before Thanksgiving and despite the Arizona sun brightening the sky, Dominic's mood was still dark. He, along with his sister and Nick, still waited for Marta to show progress.

Still very weak and fighting an infection that stubbornly resisted the first round of antibiotics, her current condition raised more questions than answers. The bouts of consciousness she experienced were brief and accentuated just how weak and tired she was.

Passing Agda in the hallway on his way to sit with their mother, he asked, "Any change?"

Agda had slept in their mother's room in case she awoke during the night. The eternal optimist, Agda smiled. "I think she looks better. She was awake for a little while, but she didn't say much. I did manage to get a little smile out of her."

"Did you get a chance to talk to the doctor?"

Yawning, she shook her head. "Not the doctor, but the nurse said that Mom was responding to the antibiotics and we should begin seeing improvement soon."

Dominic patted his sister on the shoulder. "Go back to Mom's apartment. Get some sleep. I'll sit with Mom, and I'll call you when there's some news."

"Dom, you need to come back to Mom's and get some sleep too. I know her place is tiny, but it's not good for you to keep sleeping in the family waiting area. You're not going to be any good to Mom if you're exhausted."

He knew she was right, but he couldn't leave, not until he knew that his mother was all right. Being uncomfortable was a small price to pay.

Dominic heard his name and opened his eyes. He must have dozed off. Moving his neck from side to side to work out the kinks, he looked over at his mother's bed.

"Hi, honey. Why are you sleeping in that chair?"

Springing forward out of the chair, he immediately went to his mother's bedside. "You're awake. How do you feel? Do you need anything? Do you want me to call the nurse?"

Marta smiled at her son and gently patted his hand. "I'm a little tired, but other than that, I feel fine."

Dominic breathed a sigh of relief. This was the most she had spoken—and the most responsive—since she was admitted to the hospital.

"Are you hungry? Let me get you something to eat."

Marta nodded. "That would be good. I am a little hungry."

Dominic called the nurse to see if his mother could have something to eat. It was past dinnertime, but the nurse did manage to get her some soup, crackers, and applesauce.

Dominic helped his mother as she ate a few spoonfuls of soup. She only ate a little, but it was encouraging. He even coaxed her to eat a little of the applesauce from her dinner tray. "You need to build up your strength," he said encouragingly.

After she ate, Dominic pulled his chair closer to her bedside.

"You gave us a pretty big scare."

Marta smiled. "Trust me, it wasn't intentional."

"When you get out of here, Agda is going to stay with you for a while. And when you're up to it, I'd like for you to come to Columbus."

"We'll see," she said. "One day at a time, okay?"

Dom nodded.

Marta noticed her son's haggard appearance, unshaven face, and disheveled clothing. He looked so tired. "Honey, have you been sleeping here?"

"Sort of."

"Not tonight. There's plenty of room for everyone at my apartment. You know the sofa in the living room lets out into a bed. I can't bear to think of you sleeping in a chair or on a couch in the hospital's lounge. There are more than enough people here to look after me. You need to go, get some rest, and take care of yourself."

Dominic smiled. His mother must be feeling better. She was already back to giving orders.

"How is Ilsa? Did she come with you?"

Dominic hesitated before answering. "No, she had, she couldn't, uh, she—"

"Was a fool and should have been here days ago."

CHAPTER THIRTY-SEVEN

Dominic turned quickly toward the doorway. For a brief moment, he wondered if he could trust what he was seeing: Ilsa standing there holding a vase containing a small bouquet.

She stepped into the room and placed the small vase on the bedside table. She slipped her hand in Dominic's and squeezed gently as she bent down to place a kiss on Marta's cheek.

"I'm happy to see you," Marta remarked.

"Not as happy as I am to see you," Ilsa exclaimed with a smile.

Marta commented on and thanked Ilsa for the flowers. She remarked how nice it was to have something bright and cheery to look at in her room.

After a few minutes the nurse came in to inform them that visiting hours were over, but family members could stay if they liked.

Marta had grown tired and, after a bit of coaxing, convinced Dominic to go and get some sleep.

After making sure his mother was comfortable and being once again ordered by her to leave and get some rest, Dominic and Ilsa walked out into the hallway just as she was dozing off. It wasn't until they were alone inside the elevator that he pulled her into his arms.

Ilsa could feel the weight of worry of the past days in that embrace as he melted into her arms. She held on to him as tightly as she could.

Ilsa drove them to a nearby hotel. She ordered something to eat while Dominic took a shower and changed.

He emerged from the shower feeling like a new man. Ilsa had set up their food on the room's coffee table.

"Your mother looked a little tired, but she looked good."

Dominic agreed. "This has been her best day by far. She's finally responding to the antibiotics, and the infection is clearing up." He finished his sandwich and was eyeing Ilsa's.

She pushed it toward him. It was obvious he hadn't been taking care of himself. When she saw him sitting at his mother's bedside, her heart ached. He looked like he was carrying the weight of the world on his shoulders.

After he made quick work of his meal, he leaned back and melted into the cushions of the sofa. He couldn't ever remember feeling so tired and elated at the same time. Seeing his mother sitting up in bed, eating, and looking almost like her old self gave him a lightness in his soul that he couldn't explain. And having Ilsa here with him was more than he could have imagined.

They hadn't talked much on the ride to the hotel. For part of the ride, he had been asleep.

"Thank you for coming," he said later that night as they lay in bed in each other's arms.

"You don't have to thank me for that. I should have been here with you the whole time."

"You're here now. That's all that matters. How did you manage to get the time off from work?"

Not wanting to burden Dominic, she decided to wait to tell him everything that happened later. "That's a story for another day," she said. "Right now I want you to get some sleep."

Too tired to push for details, he agreed to wait until later for the explanation. As he drifted off to sleep with Ilsa in his arms, he felt within his heart everything was going to be all right.

Thanksgiving Day was marked with the usual trappings: turkey, stuffing, mashed potatoes, green bean casserole, and cranberry sauce. While the venue wasn't typical, no one complained or seemed to mind.

Ilsa, Dominic, Agda, and Nick crammed into Marta's hospital room balancing paper plates loaded with their Thanksgiving dinner, courtesy of the hospital's cafeteria, and regaled each other with stories of holidays past.

During dinner, Marta's doctor came in to tell her that she would likely be discharged within a few days. This gave everyone another reason to celebrate and be thankful.

That evening, back at the hotel, Dominic and Ilsa lay in bed, tired, but not yet ready to go to sleep. Instead, they stayed up talking.

"What did Lu say?"

"She told me to take all the time I need and that everything at the restaurant was fine."

"That's good to hear."

"When I get back I'm giving her two weeks off with pay. I don't know what I would have done without her and the whole staff. You can help me think of a good way to show them how much they are appreciated."

"I'd be happy to."

"Speaking of staff and work, are you ready to tell me what's going on?"

Until now, Ilsa had successfully avoided the topic, which wasn't hard since Dominic had been distracted by his mother's recovery. Whenever anyone mentioned their jobs or anything to do with work, she would cleverly steer the conversation in another direction or think of an excuse to leave the room.

"Ilsa?"

Thankful the lights were off in the room and Dominic couldn't see her face nor could she see his, she paused and took a deep breath. "I quit."

She waited patiently for Dominic to say something, but he remained quiet.

"What did Grant say?" he asked finally.

"Not much. Actually, that's not entirely true. I don't know what he said. I didn't exactly wait around for him to say anything. I told him I quit, grabbed my coat and purse, and walked out."

Again, Dominic remained silent for what felt like an excruciatingly long time. When he finally responded, she was a little surprised.

After reaching up to turn on the bedside lamp, he propped himself up on one elbow, facing Ilsa. "Good!" he exclaimed.

Blinking to adjust to the light, she tried to determine if Dominic was serious. "Good?"

"I can't tell you how many times I've wanted to suggest you leave. Between the long hours, bringing work home, dealing with Grant, and trying to protect your staff, you wouldn't have been able to hold on to your sanity much longer."

She knew he was right. Sadly, if she had been willing to admit it to herself, she would have made that move a while ago. But she had been sure she could turn things around. Ultimately, she was wrong. Working at New Hope had become drudgery that she pushed through every day, and it had taken a toll.

Dominic smiled and stroked her cheek. "You're going to land on your feet, Ilsa. You're smart, talented, passionate, and driven. We'll work it out together."

Dominic turned off the lamp and held her until she felt his body relax and heard his slow, steady breathing. He had fallen asleep holding her and reassuring her. She wanted and needed to believe that now more than ever.

Telling off the boss and quitting a job with no prospects of another may not have been her best move. However, the moment had come and gone, and there was nothing she could do now but move forward. The big question now was how? With a cache of freshly degreed talent as her competition and an ever-changing demand for multi-skilled applicants, could she even compete in a different workplace that she'd comfortably avoided for so many years? She was no longer twenty-five and, like it or not, most organizations could hire someone half her age and pay them a lot less.

Her fears and worries would have to be hers alone for now. Dominic needed her and she vowed to be there for him, not out of a sense of obligation but love.

We'll work it out together. If she ever doubted this man's love for her, she didn't now. He genuinely believed in her. Now she had to believe in herself.

CHAPTER THIRTY-EIGHT

Typically, the time between Thanksgiving and Christmas was Ilsa's favorite time of year. She loved decorating her house, baking cookies, and bingeing on Christmas movies. Everything about the holidays just seemed more special than at any other time of the year. But this year would be different. With no job and the uncertainty of where her career was heading, she wasn't exactly in the mood for Christmas cookies or watching holiday romances on television.

She and Dominic had been back for a few days. He immediately dove into work at the restaurant, getting caught up on anything that had fallen behind when he was away. Thankfully, there was very little that Lu hadn't already taken care of. They had also hired a new assistant manager, something Dominic and Lu had been talking about for a while. Lu had been instrumental in recommending and hiring someone she knew who she felt would be perfect for the position, making the process to hire move quickly and smoothly.

Everyone was busy with work and the holidays. Ilsa, on the other hand, felt like time had stopped. It felt strange not having anything to do. She'd always worked and now there was nothing that challenged her mind or gave her a sense of purpose. Since she didn't have anywhere to be, she spent her nights either at Dominic's loft, waiting for him to get home from the restaurant, or at her house organizing her pantry, de-cluttering closets, and cleaning out her basement—anything to keep busy. Tonight she was at her house, sitting with her laptop, updating her résumé.

Earlier that evening, she had scanned different job boards looking for an opportunity she hoped would ignite a spark of interest, something that would be professionally challenging and at the same time fuel her enthusiasm for helping others. Maybe even eventually reigniting the passion she once enjoyed while working at New Hope. Sadly, her search hadn't produced anything that even remotely piqued her interest. It didn't help that most companies weren't posting many new jobs outside of retail and IT until the first of the year. It was a good thing she had money tucked away in her savings which would give her time to find what she truly wanted.

That, however, was the big mystery. What did she want? Corporate jobs were out, leaving several other fields to explore. If she wanted something different, she would have to think outside of the box to determine where her skills fit best. This wasn't easy, and, as much as she tried, she kept straying back to the same type of positions. When it came down to it, she knew she still wanted to work for a non-profit.

As she updated her profile on a professional networking site, she hoped she would have some luck connecting with former colleagues and acquaintances there. Unfortunately, there wasn't much success there either. So far, the only people wanting to make a connection were recruiters looking to fill positions that she wasn't remotely qualified for or interested in.

Closing her laptop, she decided to give it a rest for now. Her résumé was as good as it was going to be under the circumstances. Whoever said it was easier to find a job when you already have one wasn't kidding. How was she going to explain why she quit New Hope? Somehow, quitting wasn't as satisfying as she thought it would be. In fact, the only thing that seemed to come out of leaving was that she had managed to trade one stressful situation for another. Instead of reluctantly going to a job that she liked less and less, now she was in a position where she worried about even finding a job.

Had she made a mistake? Would it have been better just to have hung in there a little longer? Would staying have made that much of a difference? Chances are it wouldn't have mattered. People like Grant don't change, but she had, and it wasn't for the better. Left with feelings of cynicism and delusion about a job she once loved, she had to find a way to undo those negative feelings and move forward.

Ilsa looked down at her phone. She had a text from Ivy who asked how she was doing. Shortly after returning from Arizona, she told her sisters about her abrupt departure. Neither of them seemed surprised and were very supportive. They made her promise to let them know if she needed anything.

Ilsa typed a quick message back to Ivy telling her she was fine and didn't need anything. To emphasize the point, she added a smiley face emoji and hit *Send*. She was mastering the art of looking and sounding fine when inside she was anything but.

Ilsa checked her watch. Denita was late. Thinking she had gotten tied up at the office, Ilsa checked her messages, but there was nothing new.

It felt good to be out. Other than going to the grocery store and back and forth to Dominic's, she hadn't been anywhere in days. She was glad when Denita had called to invite her to lunch.

"Hey." Denita arrived windblown and bundled up against the biting wintry wind.

"I ordered you some hot tea."

After the waitress took their orders, Denita slid an envelope across the table.

"What's this?"

"Open it."

Inside the envelope was a Christmas card featuring a sexy, shirtless Santa with a silly joke about rewarding bad behavior.

"My annual cheesy Christmas card. How could I forget?"

Very little about Denita could be considered traditional, including the type of Christmas cards she chose for her friends. Every year, Denita picked out the goofiest or cheesiest card she could find. They always made Ilsa smile. This year's card was no exception.

Placing the card in her purse, Ilsa thanked her friend.

Pleased to see Ilsa smile, Denita broached another topic hoping to keep the mood light. "Are you and Dominic doing anything special for Christmas?"

Ilsa crossed her arms and thought about Denita's question before answering. Had she been so preoccupied with her own issues that she had forgotten this was their first Christmas together? "We haven't talked about it. Honestly, I haven't given it much thought."

"I find that a little hard to believe. This is your favorite time of year. I know with everything that's going on it won't be quite the same, but you should still celebrate."

"Yeah, I guess."

Ilsa was no longer smiling and Denita could see the worry on her face. She could tell Ilsa was trying to keep up a brave front and she empathized with her.

"I haven't mentioned this to anyone, but I've sent out a bunch of résumés and I haven't heard back from anyone. I know this is a tough time of year to be job hunting, but to receive nothing back is kind of disheartening. I even sent feelers out to some of the agencies New Hope worked with in the past. At least a few people called me back, but it wasn't good news. No one in the non-profit field is hiring right now."

"Look, it hasn't been that long. Things will look up. It's okay to give yourself some time off. There is no need to rush back into things. I know this is going to sound strange, but for years most of your time and energy was tied up in your work at New Hope. It was how you saw yourself. Essentially, it was your professional identity. You're going to feel out of balance for a while. That's okay, and it's perfectly normal. Allow yourself time to grieve over the way things ended, regardless of how they ended. But don't stay in that place for too long."

"Grief, huh? I don't know if I'm grieving, but I am feeling a lot of other things."

"You're allowed to be angry. Not that you need it, but you have my permission to be sad, mad, disappointed, or all of the above. Cry, scream, shout, break something. Do whatever you need to do to come out of this better, stronger, and more fierce than ever before."

Reluctantly, Ilsa nodded, not because she agreed, but she acknowledged what Denita was saying. "I'm not quite there yet, but you're right, I guess. As many women as I've counseled about working through drastic changes in their lives, you would think I'd handle this better. The fact is, I'm not. Maybe if I could figure out what stage second-guessing myself falls under, then I could move forward. I feel like the only thing that came out of my quitting was that I let Grant win."

"No, Grant didn't win. You did when you stood up and let him know that you had had enough. Don't dwell on the past. Figure out what you want your future to look like and go for it." Denita looked at her friend and winked. "Sis, you made a bold move. Now own it."

CHAPTER THIRTY-NINE

Lu peeked into Dominic's office just as he finished a call with his mother. She was still in Arizona with Agda, but the two of them would be leaving for California within the next week. Sometime after the first of the year, she would be coming to stay with Dominic for a while. Each day she was getting stronger and stronger. He couldn't have been more relieved or thankful.

"Hey, I wanted to let you know that Troy is doing a great job. I told you he would be a good hire."

"I never doubted you for a minute," Dominic responded sarcastically to Lu's obvious bragging.

"I also wanted to let you know that everything is all set for the Timpton Foundation luncheon tomorrow."

"Did you order the flowers?"

Lu walked in and sat down. "Yes. They'll be delivered around noon. I scheduled extra staff through the first of the year, so we should be set for all of the holiday parties. Also, when you get a chance, take a look at the menu suggestions for New Year's Eve and let me know what you think."

"I will." Staring intently at his computer monitor, Dominic was only partially listening.

"Do you need any help with anything? You look befuddled."

Dominic looked at Lu and shook his head. "Befuddled? Your vocabulary is as impressive as it is amusing."

"What are you working on?"

Dominic sighed. "I've been trying to link the new POS system to our accounting software. Every time I think I have it, I find that I'm missing something. I was hoping to have this up and running by now. We've been so busy lately that I haven't had that much time to dedicate to figuring it all out. Seems like when I do get back to it, I have to start all over again because I forgot what I did the previous time."

Lu nodded. "I've been meaning to work on it too. It's something we should try to figure out. It would make payroll a lot simpler."

Dominic shook his head. "You've got a million things to do already. I don't want to make it a million and one. We may have to handle payroll the old way until things slow down after the first of the year. Maybe then I can spend the time, go through all the steps, and get this to work the way it's supposed to."

"Why don't you see if Ilsa can help."

Dominic hit a few keys on the keyboard, swore, and leaned back in his chair, exasperated. "Help with what?"

"Connecting the two systems. When we were talking at her agency's employment appreciation thing, she mentioned that she used to do all of their payroll stuff until they hired someone else to do it. So you know she at least understands payroll. Plus, remember, she was the only one who was able to figure out how to run the reports when the POS system was first installed. Maybe she wouldn't mind coming in one Saturday or a few evenings if she's not too busy."

Lu was right. He had forgotten all about Ilsa helping with the reports. It had happened completely by chance. Ilsa had been sitting in his office waiting for him to finish a report so they could go out. After several failed attempts, he became frustrated and was ready to give up. Throwing up his hands, he was convinced the program was defective. Curious, Ilsa had leaned over his shoulder and asked what he was trying to do. Before he knew it, she had kicked him out of his chair, clicked on a few screens, downloaded an add-in—which he had no idea what that was or why it was needed—and produced his report.

Dominic hadn't told Lu that Ilsa quit her job, but he thought her suggestion was a good one and couldn't have come at a better time. Why hadn't he thought of it? After all, she couldn't make more of a mess with it than he had.

The lights were off in Ilsa's house when Dominic pulled into the driveway. He had texted her earlier to say he would stop by after the restaurant closed. Maybe she had decided to go to sleep instead of waiting up.

Since returning from Arizona he noticed that she wasn't quite herself. It wasn't anything overt, just subtle changes in mood that made him wonder if she was really okay. Whenever he asked how she was feeling she'd respond with "fine" or "good" and then change the subject.

Using his key, he let himself in. Just inside the door, he was met with stacks of boxes marked Giveaway. There were at least six boxes taped closed and neatly lined up and three more partially filled boxes. Looked like Ilsa had been busy.

Hearing music coming from her bedroom, Dominic went upstairs to find the room filled with piles of clothes, shoes, and accessories.

"Hi," she said, looking from behind a stack of boxes she was carrying from her closet. "I thought I heard you come in."

Not sure if she was preparing to give away all of her clothes, he asked, "What are you doing?"

She set the boxes down and moved some dresses out of the way as she made her way to the bed. Looking around the room, she announced, "I'm organizing my closet."

"Why?"

Ilsa started to explain her rationale for reorganizing an already organized closet and why she felt a need to do so at that time. Instead, she sat down on the side of the bed and looked over at Dominic, who was still standing in the doorway, looking unsure of how to navigate his way inside the messy room.

"Because I'm tired of scanning job boards, tweaking my résumé, and cleaning and re-cleaning other parts of the house," she admitted.

Dominic found an opening and made his way inside the room to join Ilsa on the bed, being careful not to step on anything or knock over the piles of folded clothes.

She leaned her head on his shoulder. "This might sound silly, but I'm bored, I'm anxious, and I don't know what else to do with myself. I haven't had this much time on my hands—ever. I feel like if I don't stay busy, then I'll start thinking, and thinking leads to rehashing the choices I've made. That's when the little voice in my head begins strongly suggesting that I messed up and I might not be able to find another job, at least one where I'm happy."

Dominic put his arm around her shoulder. "Don't listen to that voice. Listen to this one. You did not mess up. You will find another job. You are brilliant. And you are loved, more than you know."

Dominic leaned back on the bed and carried Ilsa with him.

Turning to face him, she smiled. "What would I ever do without you?"

He kissed her. "Let's hope you never have to find out."

After helping her move most of the clothes out of the way and creating a few pathways in her bedroom, Dominic and Ilsa settled into bed. It was late, but neither of them was ready for sleep.

"You know, this will be our first Christmas together and we haven't made any plans."

"What kind of plans?" she asked.

"I don't know. I think we should do something special. How about a party?"

"Seriously? With everything going on at the restaurant, when would you have the time or energy?"

"I'll make time. Besides, we can do it together. It doesn't have to be elaborate—just a few friends and some good food and wine. You can even help me decorate the loft. I usually don't even bother getting a tree, but if you're willing to help me, I will this year."

Not getting the reaction he wanted, he continued. "Come on. It'll be fun. I promise."

"Is this your way of giving me something to do besides cleaning my house?"

"Am I that obvious?"

"Glaringly."

"So is that a yes?"

"It's a strong maybe."

"I'll take it!"

CHAPTER FORTY

Dominic was still asleep when Ilsa tiptoed to the kitchen. Sitting at her kitchen table waiting for the coffee to brew, she opened her laptop to check her email. Other than spam, there was nothing worthwhile.

As she began to prepare breakfast, she tamped down the negative thoughts reminding her that the journey to a new career may be long and disappointing. *Be patient.*

For breakfast, she made bacon, fried potatoes and onions, grits, scrambled eggs, and toast. She liked cooking for Dominic almost as much as she liked cooking with him. Normally she wouldn't prepare such a large breakfast, but this morning she was using cooking as therapy.

Feeling his presence even before she saw, Ilsa turned to see Dominic standing in the doorway, barefoot, unshaven, and smiling. He always managed to look so yummy in the mornings.

"You're in a good mood."

Coming up behind her, Dominic wrapped his arms around her waist and kissed the side of her neck. "That's what waking up beside you does for me."

"I thought it was because you smelled bacon."

"That too," he said, and plucked a piece of bacon off the tray.

Dominic helped Ilsa carry the food to the table. As he was devouring a second helping of potatoes and onions, he remembered there was something he wanted to ask Ilsa. "Do you remember when you helped me run the inventory reports out of our new POS system?"

"Yes."

"Do you think you could come to the restaurant and help me with something else? I've been trying to figure it out, and nothing I do seems to work."

Ilsa put her fork down and looked over at Dominic. "Dom, am I that pitiful that you feel as if you have to keep thinking of things for me to do to keep busy?"

"No," he remarked, defensively. "It's not that at all. The truth is I legitimately need some help."

Once he explained what he needed, Ilsa apologized. "Sorry, I overreacted. I need to get it together. Yes, I'd be happy to help. How about tomorrow? I can't make any promises, but I'll take a look."

After they finished breakfast and lingered over coffee, Ilsa and Dominic began planning for their Christmas party. Taking notes, helping to decide on the food, and picking out the Christmas playlist unexpectedly lightened her mood a little.

Dominic told her he didn't have any Christmas ornaments, so she made a note to go out later that afternoon to start shopping for some before dropping off the boxes of donations to charity. She also needed to put her room back in order. Enough with the reorganizing.

After Dominic left for work, Ilsa started working in her room. Once things were back in order, she took a few minutes to email her résumé and cover letter to an agency Denita told her might be looking for a new director. Feeling accomplished when she finished, she headed to a local craft store to look for decorations to take to Dominic's.

Not sure of Dominic's taste in ornaments, she decided to pick items to create a winter wonderland theme. Looking through bins of snowmen, sparkling snowflakes, and other knickknacks, it didn't take long to find what she needed. Thinking she might decorate his Christmas tree in silver, blue, and white, she searched for but could not find enough of the silver bulbs and wondered if there were more in the stockroom.

Spotting one the store's employees stocking shelves at the end of the aisle, Ilsa got the young lady's attention.

Recognizing Ilsa and standing to greet her, the young lady smiled broadly. "Hi, Miss Tanner."

Surprised to see one of the clients from New Hope, Ilsa greeted her with a smile. "Tia! Hi. How are you? I didn't know you worked here."

"I just started a few weeks ago. It's better hours and more money than where I was working before. Now I only have to work one job."

Ilsa was curious and wanted to know how she was doing and if she was still with her boyfriend. She also wanted to know if she had completed the computer training, but she hesitated. What if she heard something she didn't like? There was nothing she could do about it.

"I've been wanting to call you, but I was kind of embarrassed. I had something I wanted to tell you."

"I'm sorry, Tia, I no longer work at New Hope. You'll have to call and talk to someone else."

"Oh. That's too bad. I wanted to tell you that you helped me figure out some things for myself."

Surprised, Ilsa didn't think Tia had been receptive to anything she'd said.

Tia leaned in, making sure no one else could hear. "The last time I was in your office, I kind of knew I was making a mistake by going back with my boyfriend. It was an even bigger mistake moving back in with him."

Ilsa wanted to stop her but at the same time was curious as to what happened.

"At first everything was fine. Then he started asking me why I was taking classes. He said it was a waste of time and that nobody would hire me even if I did finish. I don't know why I stopped going to class, but I guess it was because I believed him. I let him get in my head."

"So, what happened?"

"It didn't take long for me to figure out that he didn't care about me the same way I cared about him. I think he was only interested in how much money I could give him. Eventually, I moved out. If I hadn't, he would have kicked me out again. I didn't want to keep living like that."

Tia paused a while before continuing. "I remembered what you said, that it's not selfish to take care of myself. So that's what I'm doing now. I got this job and my own place—nothing fancy, but it's mine and nobody can take it away from me."

Ilsa was genuinely happy for Tia, who appeared more relaxed and confident than she had been the last time they talked. "So what happened with the classes?"

"I wish I could say that I finished, but I didn't. I was doing good in those classes, too. We even had a chance to shadow some people who had completed the program. That's when I started to believe that I could finish. I talked to the instructor to see if there was any way to make up the classes I had missed. She said I couldn't because I had missed too many already, but I could start again in January. This time I'm going to finish. It's one of the goals I set for myself. Something I learned to do at New Hope," she added.

"That's good to hear. I know you'll do well especially since it sounds like now you know it too."

After their conversation, Tia helped Ilsa find what she was looking for. And before she left, Tia hugged and thanked her.

That night as Ilsa lay in bed, she thought about her conversation with Tia. Happy that things were looking up for her, Ilsa realized it was time she followed her own advice.

CHAPTER FORTY-ONE

Ilsa had spent the better part of her morning at the women's shelter helping to sort and wrap gifts for the residents and their children. Sylvia French, a long-time friend who ran the shelter, had called when she found out Ilsa was no longer at New Hope. She said they were in desperate need of volunteers and wanted to know if she could help.

Working side-by-side with the volunteers felt good. The shelter had received a large donation of toys, personal care items, and winter coats, hats, and gloves which all needed to be sorted, labeled, and wrapped.

Ilsa stuck her head in Sylvia's office when she was finished. She wanted to say good-bye before she left.

Sylvia rose from her desk and motioned for Ilsa to come in. "Hey, I can't tell you how much I appreciate your help. The donations we received were a blessing, but when I saw everything, I panicked and wondered how in the world we would be able to get all of this done."

"I'm glad you called," Ilsa remarked.

"What are you up to these days? Are you taking some much-needed time off between jobs?" Sylvia asked.

Ilsa smiled awkwardly. "Not exactly. I didn't leave New Hope to go somewhere else. I just quit."

Sylvia nodded. "I see. That makes sense now. I was wondering what was going on over there. I swear, lately every time I call there's somebody new. Folks aren't returning phone calls, paperwork keeps getting lost, and I don't think anyone is checking emails. And every time I turn around, there's a new process we're supposed to be following. Sounds like you may have jumped from a burning ship, just in the nick of time."

Ilsa was sad to hear that things weren't going well at New Hope. Even though there was nothing she could do about it, she hated that everything she and the staff had built appeared to be going up in flames.

When Ilsa arrived at YiaYia's Table, the parking lot was packed. It was that time of year. People loved going out to eat around the holidays.

Once inside, she looked around for Dominic or Lu. She saw Lu first.

"Hi," she greeted Ilsa.

"The place is packed today."

"We're busy every day. It's always like this around the holidays. From the time we open until the last guests leave, we are in constant motion. I love it!"

Ilsa could see why Dominic trusted Lu with the restaurant. She had a ton of enthusiasm and was so good with the customers and staff. Ilsa could tell she loved the restaurant as much as Dominic did.

"Dominic is in his office."

Ilsa walked back to Dom's office. He was on the phone and filling out something at the same time, which he handed to Milo who was standing beside his desk. With paper in hand, Milo said hello and smiled awkwardly on his way out. After all this time, he still couldn't look Ilsa in the eye.

Completing his phone call, Dominic rose from his desk and greeted Ilsa with a kiss.

"Hungry? I can get you something from the kitchen."

"No, I had something a little earlier. A friend of mine who runs the women's shelter called me this morning. She was looking for volunteers, and I went over to help. Afterward, they gave us lunch."

"And?" Dominic could tell Ilsa had something else on her mind.

"And she told me something about New Hope that bothered me. Sounds like things are a mess over there." Ilsa didn't want to go into details. She just wanted to put it out of her mind completely. She tried to smile, but it wasn't genuine. "I know, it's not my problem."

"Hey, I get it. You put a lot of yourself into helping to make New Hope successful. To see things going downhill can't be easy. But don't let it weigh you down. Grant created this mess; he's going to have to fix it."

Resigning herself to the inevitable truth that she was out of the picture and there was nothing she could do at this point, she decided to focus on what she could control: her own life.

"So what am I doing?" she asked.

Dominic gave her his chair and pulled up the two programs. After explaining how they were supposed to work and what he had already tried, he showed her the instructions he had printed off and left her to the task of performing miracles.

After about an hour, Dominic came back to check on Ilsa. Staring intently at the monitor, she looked puzzled.

"No luck?" he asked.

"Yes and no. I just got off the phone with the software company's help desk, which proved to be very little help. But I think I may have figured it out. Give me a little more time, and I'll let you know."

Lu came in and told Dominic he was needed in the kitchen.

Before he left, he placed a plate of *kourabiedes*, Greek butter cookies, on the desk along with a cup of tea. "Brain food," he said on his way out the door.

It was another hour before Dominic rejoined Ilsa. This time she looked pleased.

Coming around to look at what was on the monitor, Dominic wasn't sure if Ilsa had solved the problem or not.

"Okay, it took me a little while to figure it out, but the programs are now talking to each other." She opened up the accounting program and made a serious of clicks. "When you get here," she instructed, "make sure this is open. I created a folder to store each week's payroll report. When you're ready to run it, click here."

"I did that before," Dominic protested.

Amused, Ilsa replied, "No, you didn't. I'll show Lu what I did, so she'll know too."

Ilsa leaned back in Dom's comfy office chair and smiled, pleased that she was able to figure out the problem.

Sitting on the side of the desk, he couldn't help but be impressed. "I honestly don't know how you figured that out. I've been working on it for weeks. You're amazing."

"Full disclosure, I did an internet search when I kept getting the same error message over and over. I thought someone else probably had the same issue and had already figured it out. Turns out, I was right."

Ilsa stood and grabbed her coat and purse. Dominic had to get back to work, and she would see him later that evening to help decorate his loft for the upcoming Christmas party. There were still a few things she needed to pick up to add to the decorations, so she needed to be on her way.

Dominic helped her with her coat and turned her around to face him. "Well, I think you're amazing." He kissed her good-bye.

Ilsa smiled mischievously. "Oh yeah? If you think that was amazing, just wait until you get home tonight."

CHAPTER FORTY-TWO

An eclectic mix of Christmas tunes—from Donny Hathaway and Bruce Springsteen to classic Brenda Lee and Nat King Cole—filled the loft as Dominic and Ilsa turned his home into a festive space filled with lights, tinsel, and sparkles. It was late when they finished, having gotten a late start. Remembering Ilsa's final words when she left the restaurant earlier, Dominic had been distracted all evening. Once through the door they had quickly dispensed with their clothes and headed straight to his bedroom, leaving the task of decorating until later.

"What do you think?" Ilsa asked, admiring their handiwork.

Joining her in front of the enormous Fraser fir they had picked out a few days ago, Dominic was pleased. With its silvery-green needles decorated in the silver, blue, and white ornaments and white sparkling lights Ilsa had purchased, it was the perfect focal point in the spacious loft.

Inhaling the wonderful wintry fragrance, Ilsa felt happier than she had in weeks. She had made up her mind to enjoy the holiday season, despite her present circumstances. Besides, she felt lately she had been doing way too much wallowing in self-pity and not enough reflecting on what was good in her life.

Dominic turned off the lights to get the full effect of the tree's twinkling lights. "Beautiful," he said.

"Don't you just love it?"

"I love you," he replied playfully.

Taking a seat and motioning for Dominic to join her, she pulled up the list for the party. Everything was checked off and ready to go. They only needed to set up the food, wine, and extra tables and chairs.

Dominic took the list out of Ilsa's hand and placed it on the coffee table. "Stop looking at that."

"I want to make sure we haven't forgotten anything," she protested.

"Tomorrow our friends will be here, enjoying delicious food, drinking great wine, and having a good time. I guarantee no one will know or care if we forgot something."

"You're right."

"I know."

Ilsa playfully punched him, and he pulled her into his arms.

"How are you doing?" he asked.

"I'm fine," she answered a little quicker than she had intended.

They had stopped talking about her job search even though it was always in the back of Ilsa's mind. She told him she'd start looking again at the beginning of the year, although she still occasionally sent out a cover letter and résumé to agencies within the area in case something came up. Recently, she had even interviewed for a position as a corporate trainer, something she hadn't shared with Dominic. While she had been excited to have been granted an interview, she knew five minutes into it that neither the job nor the company were right for her.

It felt weird not sharing that with Dominic, and she didn't exactly know why she kept it a secret. He had been nothing but supportive, which made her feel worse about keeping things from him.

As she sat wrapped in his arms, she thought about how lucky she was to have Dominic in her life. Everything about him was special. His thoughtfulness, how attentive he was toward her, his sense of humor, and his feelings for her. There was no doubt in her mind that he loved her unconditionally. She needed to love him the same.

—ele—

The Christmas party was a hit. They had been a little worried about the snow that had been steadily falling since early afternoon, but it didn't seem to deter the partygoers.

Most of the people at the party were Dominic's friends, but Denita and Cam were also there. Lu even popped in toward the end.

After the last guest left, Dominic and Ilsa met in the middle of the floor and breathed a sigh of relief.

"That was a lot of fun. Now let's go to bed and clean up tomorrow."

Ilsa looked around to assess the amount of work needed to get the loft back into shape. "There's not that much to do. If we do it tonight, we won't have to worry about it tomorrow."

Dominic frowned. What she said made sense, but he didn't want to clean. He wanted to get Ilsa into his bed and in his arms.

She had been an exceptional and charming hostess, making everyone feel welcome and being attentive to everyone's needs. And she looked incredibly beautiful doing it. Wearing a striking red jumpsuit that showed off her curvaceous figure and long legs, she accessorized the outfit with dangling gold earrings, a simple gold necklace, and a touch of red lipstick that pulled the whole look together. Dominic practically drooled every time she walked by.

"Come here," he said as she passed by carrying a tray of dirty wine glasses.

"We're supposed to be cleaning," she protested half-heartedly.

"I know, but I'd rather do this," he said, taking the tray and placing it on a nearby table. He then pulled her to him and kissed her tenderly on the lips. "Listen," he said. "They're playing our song."

Ilsa giggled. "We don't have a song."

"Maybe we should," he said swinging her around.

"Christmas Time is Here" by the Vince Guaraldi Trio was playing, and because it was one of her favorite Christmas tunes, Ilsa conceded and remained in Dominic's arms as they continued to dance.

"You look beautiful tonight."

"Thank you. And might I say, you look very handsome yourself."

They continued to dance until the music ended. Waiting for the next song to begin, Dominic held Ilsa away from him. Looking into her beautiful brown eyes caused his heart to flutter and his mind to wander to places that only existed in his dreams. There was so much he wanted to say to her, but he couldn't seem to organize his thoughts. He wished he could properly put into words how much she meant to him and how full his heart was at that moment. But there were no words, no song or gesture sufficient enough to convey the intensity of love he felt for her.

"What?" she asked playfully. Convinced he was trying to get out of cleaning, she reached up to kiss him on the cheek, picked up the tray of glasses, and carried them to the kitchen.

Unable to move, Dominic remained still for a few seconds longer, regretting not having spoken those words he wanted her to hear. The music started again. As Mariah Carey sang "All I want for Christmas is you," Dominic closed his eyes and exhaled slowly. Once he trusted his legs to move, he began helping Ilsa straighten up, but not before he slipped the ring back in his pocket.

CHAPTER FORTY-THREE

"Merry Christmas, baby."

Dominic awakened to Ilsa standing at the side of the bed holding a breakfast tray.

"What's this?" he asked groggily.

"It's breakfast in bed for my man," she remarked.

Sitting up in bed and taking the tray from Ilsa, he eyed the contents hungrily. Waffles, sausage links, fresh fruit, and hot coffee. All of his favorites. "I like the sound of that."

"Which part?" she asked, climbing into bed beside him and grabbing a couple of grapes off his tray.

"The part where you call me your man. Sounds very old-school and sexy."

"Speaking of..."

She reached over the side of the bed and retrieved a gift bag. "Merry Christmas."

"What? Breakfast in bed and gifts? This is too much." Dominic pulled the tissue paper out of the bag and looked inside. He threw his head back and laughed. "Fuzzy dice! These will look great in Bella."

"But wait, there's more," she announced. She reached over the side of the bed again and retrieved another gift bag, then a large wrapped box, and, finally, a smaller wrapped box. "Open that one last," she instructed, pointing to the box.

"Seriously, Ilsa. You didn't have to—"

She stopped him before he could continue. "I know. I wanted to. It's what you do when you love someone, right?"

Dominic unwrapped the large box first. Inside was a pale yellow cashmere sweater that Ilsa knew would look good with his coloring. Then he opened a gift bag to find a collection of skincare products for men by her lotions and potions lady. When Dominic started to open the last box, he looked over at Ilsa who was trying to keep a straight face but failing miserably.

Tearing off the last piece of paper, he realized he then had to pull a bunch of tape off the box. Inside the box was more tissue paper. "You're making me work hard for this," he said. When he finally reached the contents, he pulled them out. It didn't register at first until he saw exactly what Ilsa had given him. "It's the complete set of *Rocky* movies."

Ilsa was beaming. "Notice anything else?"

Examining the set of movies more closely, he exclaimed, "They're signed! Sylvester Stallone signed them!"

She nodded. "Do you like them?"

Dominic broke into a wide grin. "This is amazing! Yes, I love them. How? When?"

Ilsa couldn't stop smiling. "I wanted to get you something extra special, and you told me on our first date that you liked the *Rocky* movies."

"How? Where?" he asked, clearly at a loss for words.

Eager to tell the story, she said, "I read where Sylvester Stallone was going to be at Keystone Comic Con. I've always seen pictures of celebrities at those things, and I found out that people bring stuff for them to autograph all the time. I thought I would take a chance and see if he would be willing to sign my memorabilia. This was my first comic con, so I didn't exactly know what to expect."

"You drove over seven hours to Philly? When? Wh—"

Ilsa nodded. "Denita went with me. Turns out there's a cute little winery on the way. That's how I got her to go with me."

Dominic was speechless. This had to be the most thoughtful gift anyone had ever given him.

Careful not to overturn his breakfast tray, she leaned over and kissed Dominic. Resting her forehead against his, she said, "I love you very much. You make me very happy, and I want to do the same for you."

Dominic set his presents aside. He opened the drawer of his nightstand and pulled out an envelope. Presenting it to Ilsa, he said, "Merry Christmas."

Eyeing him suspiciously, she took the envelope. What she found inside brought a smile to her face. "A spa day!" She closed her eyes and imagined a full day of pampering at one of the city's premier spas. "A mani, pedi, and hot stone massage. I can't wait! Thank you!"

He smiled. "I have something else. Look under your pillow."

Puzzled, Ilsa did as instructed. From underneath her pillow, she pulled out a small velvet pouch. Cautiously, she opened the pouch, revealing diamond stud earrings. Surprised and pleased, she turned to Dominic. "Ohhh," she exclaimed excitedly. "They're beautiful. Wait, are these from the little jewelry shop in the Short North?"

He nodded.

"How did you know? I was thinking about buying these but thought I should spend my money on something more practical."

One evening on their way to a movie, Ilsa had stopped by the jewelry store to pick up a necklace she'd had repaired. While she was waiting, he noticed her looking at the diamond earrings. Once he figured out which pair she liked, he made a point of going back to buy them. The first time he saw them, he thought the sparkling round diamonds set in white gold would look stunning on her.

"Thank you, Dom. This is one of the best Christmases I've had in a long time. It's not because of the presents—they're nice, very nice. It's more about spending this time together that's made it so nice."

He felt the same.

Spending the rest of the day watching Christmas movies and sharing a nice dinner they prepared together, Dominic couldn't remember being happier. But he continued to wrestle with a question that weighed heavily on his mind. Afraid, he never brought it up. Another time, he reasoned. He wanted to ensure their first Christmas together wouldn't be their last.

CHAPTER FORTY-FOUR

Ilsa had decided to spend a few days in Cincinnati with her family after Christmas. She promised Dominic she would be back so they could spend New Year's Eve together.

Pulling into the driveway of her parents' home immediately transported her back to her childhood. The outside of the house was decorated with colorful lights with a lighted candle in each window. A few years back, her father had swapped out the old candles for new LED models at his grandchildren's insistence.

Feeling very nostalgic, she remembered how special Christmas was when she and her sisters were growing up. She and Ivy loved baking Christmas cookies with their mother. Imani, not so much. Imani liked decorating the tree and meticulously placed the ornaments in a way that no two colors, styles, or characters were ever near each other.

Ilsa and her father were in charge of decorating the outside of the house. They would string lights across the porch railing and along the frame of the house, and sometimes they framed each window with strings of lights. It was a lot of hard work, something her sisters hated but Ilsa enjoyed.

Regardless of their roles in helping to make Christmas special, Ilsa and her sisters loved being together this time of year. As their families grew, it became harder to all be in the same place at one time, but they still did whatever they could to make it work.

Stepping into her parents' house, Ilsa called out. "Hello. Is anybody home?"

Virgil was the first to come from the kitchen to greet his daughter, wrapping her in a tight hug. "Hey, sweetheart. Your mother is fixing lunch. Perfect timing."

Ilsa's mother stuck her head out of the kitchen and called out to her daughter, "Hi, baby. Come into the kitchen. I'm cooking."

Ilsa and her father stepped into a warm kitchen filled with so many delicious aromas, her mouth started to water.

Ruby's hands were covered in flour. Holding her hands up and out of the way, she crossed the room and kissed her daughter on the cheek. "Have a seat at the table with your father. Everything will be ready in a few minutes."

Ilsa did as instructed after her offer to help was denied. "I have some gifts in the car for you. I'll bring them in a little later. And Dominic told me to tell you hello." Ilsa placed a box on the table. "He sent these for you too."

Peeking inside the box, Virgil licked his lips. "Ooh, pastries."

Ilsa got up and poured herself a cup of coffee. "He got up early this morning and made them before he went to the restaurant."

Ilsa saw Ruby and Virgil exchange glances. "I mean, he told me he got up to make them."

Ilsa sat down across from her father. "Honey, you're an adult, and we are not that old-fashioned. How and where you and Dominic spend your time together is your business. You don't have to censor your comments for us."

"Yeah," she said slowly, "That's going to take a little getting used to."

As she enjoyed lunch with her parents, Ilsa got up to speed on all the latest gossip, drama, and news from the neighborhood and within her family.

"Is Dominic's mother still doing well?" Ruby asked.

"Yes, I spoke to her a few days ago. She sounded strong and was happy to be with her daughter and grandkids in

California. She's supposed to be coming sometime after the first of the year to spend some time with Dominic. She's a strong-willed lady. I'm sure eventually she'll be going back to Arizona and her life there."

Clearing the dishes and leftover food from the table, both Ruby and Virgil worked together, again forbidding Ilsa to help. Sipping a cup of tea, she watched as her parents put the food away and loaded the dishwasher. What would appear to be an ordinary daily task to some actually gave her a glimpse into their relationship, something she hadn't paid much attention to before now.

As she continued to watch, she paid attention to their subtle gestures and interactions. For instance, the way her father stroked her mother's arm when he joined her at the sink to wash a pan. The kiss he placed on the back of her neck when helping her untie her apron. The compliments about the wonderful meal she had prepared, even though she must have cooked thousands of meals throughout their marriage. It was all of those things coupled with the little touches and smiles and the gentle way they spoke to each other that warmed her heart. It was easy to see how much love they had for each other. A solid love that had stood the test of time.

Her father once told her that he knew he had found the love of his life in her mother. Curious, Ilsa had asked how he knew. He started by admitting he had wasted a lot of time at first playing it safe and not taking his relationship seriously. But once he appreciated how special Ruby was, he stopped playing around. It was because, he'd said, he had found someone who made his worst days better and his best days extraordinary. He also added that with Ruby, he stopped running away from forever, knowing she would be a part of it.

That evening, the Dixon house was filled with family, laughter, noise, and good food as they celebrated a second Christmas. A few neighbors had even stopped by to join in the festivities. The more, the merrier.

"I like second Christmas," exclaimed Ivy's youngest son as he opened his gifts from his aunts and grandparents.

"Don't get used to this," Ivy warned. "We're only doing this because it's the first time we could all get together."

Nonetheless, all the nieces and nephews reacted to the bonus holiday with the same joy and enthusiasm as the first.

Meeting her sisters in the kitchen while their parents doted on their grandkids, Ilsa was happy for the brief reprieve.

"I have to agree with the kids. I like the second Christmas too. Why only have one day of presents, food, and fun when you can have two?"

"Trust me, one is plenty," Ivy remarked. "The thought of extending Christmas over two days gives me hives."

"No Dominic this time?" Imani asked, changing the subject.

Ilsa shook her head. "He's been pretty busy at the restaurant with the holidays and all."

Ivy poured herself a glass of wine and sat down across from Ilsa. "I notice something sparkly on your ears. Is that courtesy of Mr. Wonderful?"

Imani swooped in to take a look. "Ooh, those are nice. From Dominic?"

"Yes, for Christmas."

"Things seem to be getting serious between you two."

Ilsa looked at Imani. "Why, because he bought me diamond earrings?"

"No, because of how much time you spend together, the dreamy look you get when you talk about him, and the way the two of you are when you're together," Ivy explained.

"You've seen us together a total of one time."

"That was all I needed. You forget everything you tell us about your relationship when we talk. Why are you being defensive?"

Annoyed by Imani's persistent interest in her relationship, Ilsa replied, "I'm not. Why are you pushing this?"

"I hope you're not still holding Dominic at arm's length. It's easy to see he loves you and I know you love him, even if I've only seen the two of you together one time," Imani added sarcastically. "You need to dive in with both feet and start building your future with this man. Stop acting as if you have all the time in the world."

"What's the rush? Besides, wasn't it you who told me to protect my heart?"

"I didn't say to keep it under lock and key. Anyway, that was before I recognized how much being in love changed you, in a good way."

Refusing to get caught up in her sister's assessment of Ilsa's love life, this time it was Ivy who changed the subject. "So how are things going with you? Any new job prospects?"

"Not really. I decided to start looking again more seriously in January. Not many companies are hiring right now anyway."

Ivy agreed. "So what are you doing with all of your free time since you're not working?"

"Not much. I've volunteered a few times at the women's shelter, and Dom needed help at the restaurant with some accounting software he couldn't get to work. Other than that, I'm just trying to stay positive."

"How's that working?" Ivy asked.

"To be honest, I still throw myself the occasional pity party, but I try to keep that at a minimum. Even though I'm working extra hard to keep up a brave front, I'm still a little worried."

"You'll be fine," Imani said.

"That's what I keep telling myself. But what happens if January comes and goes, and I still don't have a job? Like it or not, that's a reality I may have to face."

CHAPTER FORTY-FIVE

On the drive from Cincinnati, Ilsa had gotten a call from Priscilla. She told her Grant had gotten fired. Ilsa wasn't able to get too many details out of her because she had been calling from work and had to end their call when a staff member needed her help. Priscilla promised to call her in a few days with more details.

Driving down the highway, she tried to stay focused on the road and the light snow falling, but she couldn't stop thinking about what was going on at New Hope. What had Grant finally done to get fired? It must have been something pretty horrible, considering she thought he should have been fired a long time ago.

What did this mean for her, if anything? She wondered if she should leave well enough alone and continue on a different path, leaving New Hope and all the bad memories in the past behind, or...was there another alternative? The board had passed her over before for the executive director position and had picked someone who was her polar opposite. Why would they consider her this time?

Hearing about Grant's firing should have given her a sense of satisfaction. It didn't. Quite frankly, she didn't know how she felt.

She wanted to talk to Dominic. Looking at the time on her dash, she figured he would still be busy at the restaurant. They would see each other later and could talk about it then. He had a way of helping her see things clearly, which is exactly what she needed right now.

Although she had only been away for a few days, she missed Dominic. It was funny, but she hadn't realized just how much time they spent together, until they were apart. And she couldn't remember the last time she had slept alone. It felt strange.

While she was at her parents', he called every night to say goodnight. During the day she sent him text messages letting him know how much she missed him. He would respond with goofy emojis or would write something sweet to let her know how much he missed her too.

She couldn't wait to see him tonight. The topic of New Hope could wait until another day. Tonight, she decided, was going to be all about them and nothing else.

Continuing her drive, she put the conversation with Priscilla out of her head and focused on one thing: getting home to Dominic.

Ilsa was due home soon, and Dominic could hardly wait. The restaurant was closing early so the staff could enjoy some much-needed time off with family and friends. He had left Lu and Troy in charge, and he was on his way to pick up a special bottle of wine. The wine shop was out of the way, but he knew it would be worth it to have for tonight.

The snow that had fallen earlier had come as a surprise but didn't cause much concern. Ilsa had called when she left Cincinnati, so he knew approximately what time she would be home, barring any traffic or weather issues. She had assured him she would be careful on her drive back.

Tonight they were to meet at her house. The plan for the evening included the two of them preparing a nice dinner, sharing a bottle of wine, and hopefully creating some New Year's Eve memories in a bubble-filled tub.

Even though it had only been a few days, Dominic missed Ilsa while she was away. They had spoken a few times over the phone and exchanged text messages, but it wasn't the same as her being here. He missed waking up beside her. He missed her laughter and quirky sense of humor. He missed how she smelled, though he never had an opportunity to get used to just one scent. But most of all, he missed her presence, just knowing she was right there.

The plan for tonight didn't only include dinner and wine. He had bigger plans—plans that included letting Ilsa know exactly how much she meant to him and how much he enjoyed being with her. Tonight he would tell her that he loved her, even though she already knew that, but this time he planned to tell her that he didn't want to wake up another day without her next to him. He was going to say that every day was better, every sunset sweeter, and every song more special because of her. She needed to know—he planned to tell her—that before she came into his life, he had no concept of unconditional love and now he did.

Tonight, he planned to tell her all those things. And he planned to ask her to be his wife.

This time, he wasn't nervous or afraid. Just the opposite, he couldn't have been more sure. Yes, tonight was the night. Everything would be perfect.

As he focused on the details of the evening ahead, his mind and heart soared, causing him to be completely unaware of the pickup truck that ran through the stop sign.

CHAPTER FORTY-SIX

Ilsa ran from the parking lot and through the doors of the hospital's emergency department. Frantically looking around for help, she spotted the information desk.

There's been an accident. County Hospital.

Fragments of the phone call she received from someone notifying her that Dominic had been in an accident kept playing like a bad dream she couldn't shake. Fighting to keep from falling apart, she approached the help desk.

"There's been an accident. Dominic Markos. He was brought here. I need to see him." She couldn't seem to get the words out fast enough as she held on to the desk for support.

The attendant behind the desk typed something into her computer. "Are you family?"

"What?"

The attendant repeated the question. "Are you family?"

Unable to speak, she simply nodded.

The attendant took her name and typed something else into her computer, then printed a name tag. Before handing Ilsa the tag, she instructed her to wear it while she was in the hospital. "Go through those double doors and make a left at the nurse's station. Mr. Markos is still in the emergency area. Room twenty-five."

Ilsa grabbed the tag and bolted through the double doors. Once past the doors, she tried to recall where she was supposed to go from there. Then she remembered. Room twenty-five. When she reached the nurse's station, she saw room twenty-five only a few more feet ahead.

Praying with each step that Dominic was all right, she finally reached his room. Knocking gently, she heard someone say, "Come in."

Taking a deep breath, she entered the room and saw Dominic sitting on the side of the bed. She walked in and waited for the nurse to finish checking his vitals. "Everything looks good," he announced. "I'll check on those discharge papers."

Dominic was wearing a cast on one arm and had a small bandage on his forehead. Breathing a sigh of relief, Ilsa rushed to his side.

"Are you okay? Are you in pain? What happened?" she asked, wanting to hug him but afraid she might hurt him.

He nodded. "It's only a broken arm. I'm afraid my car is in worse condition than I am."

Taking his face in her hand, she felt relief wash over her. "I don't care about the car. When I got that call, my mind instantly went to the worst place. The only thing I heard was that you were in a car accident. They said you were hit by a truck. I was so scared."

With his uninjured arm, Dominic pulled her to him. "It was a pickup truck that blew through a stop sign. I'm okay. A little banged up, but okay."

Surprised by the overwhelming emotion, she stepped back and tried to put on a brave face.

Gingerly touching the bandage on his forehead, she tried to ask about it but couldn't form the words for fear she would start to cry.

Dominic took her hand. "Honestly, I'm fine. This is just a cut. I don't have a concussion. Tomorrow I'll probably be pretty sore, but the doctor has given me some pain meds to help with that."

After he was discharged and wheeled to the hospital's entrance, Ilsa brought the car around and helped him get in. When she was helping him to secure his seat belt, she noticed the blood on the front of his shirt. She hadn't noticed that before. It didn't make her queasy but again reminded her of his injuries. Swallowing the lump in her throat she steadied herself. She had to keep it together and get them both home.

"How are you feeling?" she asked, forgetting that she had already asked him the same question two other times.

"Ilsa, I'm fine. After a few pain pills and a good night's sleep, I'll be better than fine."

Once they reached the loft, Ilsa helped Dominic get out of his clothes and into bed. Taking his shirt and soaking it in the utility sink, she closed her eyes as tightly as possible, squeezing back tears.

It didn't take long for her to fix Dominic something to eat. He probably wasn't very hungry, but he needed to take his pain meds with food.

Ilsa bought Dominic his dinner on a tray and helped him get situated so he could eat.

"Some New Year's Eve celebration," he remarked.

"We were planning on having dinner together anyway. Same thing, but slightly different."

"I wanted tonight to be special."

"As far as I'm concerned, it is. Knowing that you're all right is all the special I need."

Dominic yawned. The pain meds were kicking in. It was just a matter of time before he would be fast asleep. Ilsa removed the tray and made sure he was comfortable before she left to clean up. Kissing him on the cheek, she promised to be back as soon as she finished in the kitchen.

Standing alone in the kitchen, Ilsa leaned against the wall, allowing the solid structure to support her body as she helplessly gave in to the latest wave of emotions. The kitchen had been quiet, sans the low hum of the refrigerator—that is, until the first sob broke that silence, then another, and another. This time when the tears threatened to spill over, she didn't stop them. She couldn't. This overflow of feelings mixed with relief shook her to the core as tears streamed down her face. Earlier, not wanting to show how worried, scared, and relieved she felt, she had held back the tears. Now, there was no holding back.

Whispering a prayer of thanks for protecting Dominic from dangers seen and unseen didn't feel as if it was enough. Realizing a different set of circumstances could have rendered a much more severe ending, the sobs continued, ripping free from the place that could have been. The speed of the pickup truck, icier roads, or even other cars traveling at that same time, on the same road.... Dominic's injuries could have been much more serious, and the tears she shed would have been the result of a different outcome. What she knew for sure was that the thought of losing Dominic chilled her to the bone and left her with a feeling of loss and emptiness. Never again did she want to experience that feeling.

Quickly drying her eyes, she tidied up the kitchen as best she could, lingering long enough to hide the evidence of her tears. On her way back to the bedroom, she recalled something Imani had said recently. *Stop acting as if you have all the time in the world.*

Tonight had proven that to be true. Had she been taking her relationship with Dominic for granted? Maybe this was her wakeup call.

CHAPTER FORTY-SEVEN

"Yes, Lu, I'm fine. Yes, Ilsa is taking very good care of me."

Ilsa was in the kitchen preparing lunch. Against her advice, and after only two days of rest, Dominic insisted on going to the restaurant. He asked her to drive him. She was happy to oblige. His car was totaled, and he had yet to make arrangements for a rental.

Bringing their lunch into the living room, she sat down and tried to reason with Dominic once more. "I think you should strongly consider taking one more day. Lu and Troy have everything under control. The restaurant will be fine."

"I know. I just need to check on a few things, and then I'll come back home and rest. I promise."

"Am I dropping you off or hanging around? I've seen how checking on a few things can turn into a much bigger time commitment."

"Nope, not today. You can keep me honest by coming in with me."

Dominic devoured the soup and sandwiches she had prepared and was getting ready to eat her sandwich when he noticed she hadn't touched her food. "What's wrong? Why aren't you eating?"

"Nothing is wrong. I'm just not very hungry."

"Ilsa?"

"Okay. Nothing is wrong, but there is something I've wanted to talk to you about. But with everything going on, I couldn't find a good time."

Concerned, Dominic took her hand. "Now is a good time. Tell me."

"On New Year's Eve when I was on my way back from Cincinnati, I got a call from Priscilla. She told me Grant had been fired. I didn't get a lot of details at the time because she only had a few minutes to talk."

"Did you find out what happened?"

"Sort of."

"Meaning?"

"Well, one of the board members called shortly after that, actually on New Year's Day." Ilsa paused before continuing. "They offered me the executive director position."

Cautiously elated, Dominic smiled and asked, "Is that a good thing? Is it something you want? You know I'll support whatever decision you make."

She smiled and nodded. "I think so. At one time I loved what I was doing. That only changed because Grant made it a difficult place to work."

"Did you accept the offer?"

"No, I haven't given them an answer yet. I told them to give me a few days to think about it." She took a deep breath and said, "But my answer is going to be yes, with a few conditions."

Dominic was relieved. He knew deep down this was what Ilsa wanted and where she belonged, it wasn't hard to see she was excited.

"I'm proud of you."

Ilsa felt pretty proud of herself too. She had already started to make plans. As soon as she was in her new position, she would begin the process of repairing everything Grant had attempted to destroy during his reign. It wouldn't be easy, but she wanted to make the working environment at New Hope even better than it was before. She was also planning to reach out to a few people who had recently resigned to offer them their jobs back.

"Thank you, Dom, for supporting me, encouraging me when I was down and for loving me."

Leaning in, Dominic kissed her. "You make it easy to do all of those things."

Ilsa pulled her car around to a parking space at the back of the restaurant. She linked arms with Dominic as they walked inside.

It was cold and blustery, a typical January day. The only thing Ilsa could think about after Dom finished what he needed to do at the restaurant was going back to the loft and hunkering down for the next few days.

She had decided to give New Hope a start date of two weeks out. Knowing she would be busy once she started back, she wanted to spend her remaining free time with Dominic.

She was happy—happy that she would be working and doing something she felt was important and in a place that offered new beginnings. But most of all, she was happy with the man who was at her side and in her life. This man whom she loved and couldn't imagine her life without.

Tonight, she had a special evening planne—a delicious meal, candles, music, and a heart-to-heart talk. It was time she let Dominic know how much she loved him. She also wanted to talk about their future together, whatever that looked like. It didn't matter to her as long as he was a part of it. Taking one day at a time was fine before, but now she wanted it all, especially when she knew how quickly things could change.

It was time, she had decided. Time to think about their forever, something she was no longer hesitant to imagine.

Stepping out of the cold and into the warm restaurant, Ilsa turned to go to Dominic's office.

"Wait, let's stop by the kitchen. I need to check with Milo about something, and I want you to try a new dessert Troy recommended we add to the menu."

"Ooh, I hope it's something made with chocolate."

Following Dominic down a narrow hallway and into the dining room, she turned to greet Lu.

Seeing Dominic for the first time since the accident, Lu hugged him gingerly. Letting go, she looked up at him, allowing her smile to convey what her words could not.

Lu turned to Ilsa and hugged her too. "I'm *really* happy to see you," she said with a big smile.

Lu gave Dominic a playful punch and hurried off, mumbling something about being good to go.

There seemed to be a lot of activity in the restaurant. Ilsa figured it was probably a large party having lunch at that time. She was walking toward the dining room and stopped. Her parents were there, seated at a table near the windows. Then she saw her sisters and their husbands. And Marta, Denita, and Cam.

Quickly, she turned to Dominic who didn't appear to be surprised at all.

Instead, Dominic stood facing her wearing the sweetest smile.

"What's going on?" she asked breathlessly.

"They're here for us."

Unsure of what was going on, she looked at Dom for an answer.

"Ilsa, I asked everyone here today for a special reason." He looked around the room and said, "These are the people who love us and care about us. They are here because I want them to be a part of this."

Ilsa covered her mouth with her hands. Unexpectedly, a tear rolled down her cheek and brushed her fingertips.

Standing face to face with her, Dominic wiped the tear away. "This is where I first met you. I didn't know it at the time, but I certainly felt there was something special about you even then. From that moment you caught my attention and held it. Not long after that, you captured my heart. It didn't take long before I knew that I wanted you to be part of my forever, a forever that I couldn't imagine without you."

Dominic reached in his pocket and retrieved the ring he had been holding on to for months. Taking Ilsa's hand he knelt before her.

"So I'm asking you right now, in front of our friends and family, would you make me one of the happiest men in the world and say yes to being my wife?"

And on that cold, wintry day, with warm hearts, in a room overflowing with love, Ilsa Tanner agreed to marry Dominic Markos and begin their forever.